T0013798

FARAWAY THE SOUTHERN SKY

FARAWAY THE SOUTHERN SKY

A Novel
by

Joseph Andras

Translated by Simon Leser

V E R S O
London • New York

This English-language edition first published by Verso 2024
First published as *Au loin le ciel du sud* © Actes Sud 2021
Translation © Simon Leser 2024
The publisher and translator gratefully acknowledge Nathaniel Rudavsky-Brody for permission
to quote from his translation of *Benjamin Fondane's Ulysses* (Syracuse University Press, 2017)
and PM Press for permission to reproduce the Victor Serge quotation, appearing here in
epigraph, from *A Blaze in the Desert*, edited and translated by James Brook (PM Press, 2017).
Every effort has been made to secure permission from the copyright holder for
quoted and photographic material. If anything is amiss or has been overlooked,
the publisher will endeavor to make amends at the earliest opportunity.

All rights reserved

The moral rights of the author and translator have been asserted

1 3 5 7 9 10 8 6 4 2

Verso
UK: 6 Meard Street, London W1F 0EG
US: 388 Atlantic Avenue, Brooklyn, NY 11217
versobooks.com

Verso is the imprint of New Left Books

ISBN-13: 978-1-80429-171-9
ISBN-13: 978-1-80429-173-3 (US EBK)
ISBN-13: 978-1-80429-172-6 (UK EBK)

British Library Cataloguing in Publication Data
A catalogue record for this book is available from the British Library

Library of Congress Cataloging-in-Publication Data

Names: Andras, Joseph, 1984– author. | Leser, Simon, translator.
Title: Faraway the southern sky : a novel / Joseph Andras ; translated by
   Simon Leser.
Other titles: Au loin le ciel du sud. English
Description: English-language edition. | London ; New York : Verso, 2024.
Identifiers: LCCN 2023052650 (print) | LCCN 2023052651 (ebook) | ISBN
   9781804291719 (paperback) | ISBN 9781804291733 (e-book)
Subjects: LCSH: Hồ, Chí Minh, 1890–1969—Fiction. | LCGFT: Biographical
   fiction. | Novels.
Classification: LCC PQ2701.N368 A913 2024 (print) | LCC PQ2701.N368
   (ebook) | DDC 843/.92–dc23/eng/20231213
LC record available at https://lccn.loc.gov/2023052650
LC ebook record available at https://lccn.loc.gov/2023052651

Typeset in Electra by Hewer Text UK Ltd, Edinburgh
Printed and bound by CPI Group (UK) Ltd, Croydon, CR0 4YY

TRANSLATOR'S NOTE

This book includes the work of two other translators: the Victor Serge epigraph was taken from James Brook's *A Blaze in the Desert* (PM Press, 2017); the Benjamin Fondane verses are from Nathaniel Rudavsky-Brody's *Benjamin Fondane's Ulysses* (Syracuse University Press, 2017).

The reader might find that not all the words in this translation of *Au loin le ciel du sud* (Actes Sud, 2021) were translated into English. Of those left untouched, most follow the logic by which no American should expect to be fed a London "Tube" or a Parisian "metro" in the form of a pre-chewed "subway." The rest fall in that category nosy specialists like to call a "choice." These include the word *indigène*, for which none of the usual conversions, "native" or otherwise, capture the connection to the *Code de l'indigénat*—the set of laws the French colonial empire imposed on its subjugated populations. It is accompanied by a whole host of names and acronyms whose explanations, not present in the original text (even when the French *lecteur* might not be expected to know them), threaten to weigh down the prose. A selection of them is reproduced and glossed below. The reader might enjoy browsing it now, if not as a list of the novel's ingredients, then as a slice of the French twentieth century.

Bourse du travail: literally "labor exchange:" a labor council, usually composed of local unions.

CGT: Confédération générale du travail, literally "General Confederation of Labor," a national trade union center that, prior to 1936, was strongly associated with the SFIO.

CRS: Compagnies républicaines de sécurité, literally "Republican Security Corps," the French National Police's reserve corps. They are well known today for their zealous dedication to crowd and riot control, such that any cop found in the vicinity of protesters tends to be labeled a CRS, whether or not they actually are.

Groupe des patriotes annamites: literally "Annamite Patriots Group," a collective fighting for the Vietnamese cause, formed in 1919 in Paris, of which Nguyên Tât Thanh was a founding member.

L'Humanité: newspaper founded in 1904 by Jean Jaurés, tied to the SFIO until 1920, and thereafter to the French Communist Party.

indigène: literally "native," and like the English word has plenty of colonial connotations, though these are much stronger in the French. Also a legal term directly related to the Code de l'indigénat, the oppressive system of laws that until the late 1940s maintained French rule over the colonies and their indigènes populations.

ORTF: Office de radiodiffusion-télévision française, literally

"French Radio and Television Broadcasting Office," the national agency in charge of all broadcasting in the country from 1964 to1974. A symbol, particularly after 1968, of the state's monopoly on information.

PMU: Paris mutuel urbain, the state-supervised monopoly for off-track betting and a stand-in term for the cafés-cum-bars it operates all over the country.

SFIO: Section française de l'Internationale ouvrière, literally "French Section of the Workers' International," founded in 1905 as a union of various French socialist tendencies and as an affiliate of the Second International.

Sûreté: or Sûreté générale until 1934, literally "General Security," a national police agency largely equivalent to the FBI in the United States or the Special Branch in the UK.

For Nûdem Durak, free one day

It takes men without faces,
it takes faces without men.

Victor Serge, "It Takes"

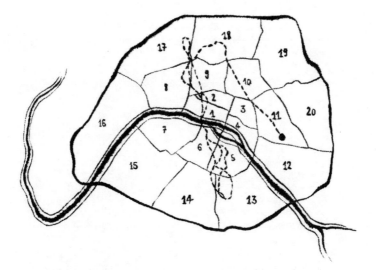

Paris, its arrondissements, and the author's journey

There is no life but in the shadows. In backlight and in the features we struggle to discern, in the silhouettes doubtful of their shapes and in the subdued, if not subjugated, glimmer. The words half-said and the haze, the galleries delved into and the embers sheltered in our hands. Great men failed it all, you think, bartering their souls for the limelight. Glory and renown's eleven letters spell the same defeat—so much blood under the pedestals of statues, such surrender on the radiant screens, so many omissions in the exalted scenes. Nothing depraves like success, once warned a Communard dear to your heart.

Hô Chí Minh the icon, revered Supreme Leader, interests you very little. Portraits printed on bank notes from a Vietnam won over by international trade, even less. You only ever cherished those at the back, the losers, the ignored, the third-rates, the fuck-ups—those there, laid low under shoddy stars, not worth even a penny.

We know the president, illustrious goatee enthroned in History somewhere between Lenin and Gandhi. Indeed, that's probably all we know: the high priest of a communism perished and everywhere denounced. But the man for whom you harbor such affection was still a moneyless vagabond. He wasn't called Hô Chí Minh, for one thing: he changed names like he changed shirts, sweating in the hope, no less, of making us all equal at last; he slept in pigsties, wrote articles in a language his mother had never sung to him in, and roamed Paris under the eyes of devious cops.

It's this man, in exile, in the nooks of a capital just out of the war, that you go in search of, knowing you won't find a thing.

A bystander taps on his mobile phone, his shoulder propped against a signpost; another passes by on a bicycle, soft wind fiddling with his shoulder-length hair. The sky's blue shows no ambition other than to ensure rooflines stick out in one, clean cut. A woman takes a drag on her cigarette, sitting in front of a laundromat, and the smoke loops ribbon-like in the black of her hair; another crosses the street—her eldest daughter, not quite a teenager, wears a dark turban and an olive-green jacket. These flâneurs lack the art of the title: a crowd of walkers and of wheels, two, four, whatever, descends, scrambles, shoves, sprawls ravenous and babbling into the city.

Paris is a monster whose teeth were whitened—some say its olden name refers, in part, either to marshes, to mud, or to mice: no doubt we should've left it at that. The city grabs at one's throat and stuffs it full of tar; the avenues, sidewalks and facades have a grim look about them, stretching with the confidence of looters or abductors. As for humid earth in

3

the morning, tall grass, nude animals, or treetops: these no longer catch the eyes of passersby. Stonework has a cleverness to it, erasing even the memory of what it took.

Somewhere on this street of one and a half kilometers (Charonne is its name), lived Nguyên Tât Thanh (his name, back then), fresh from London, and "incognito" in a bedsit. Or here, at least, is where the first signs of him point you. You owe them to an article published in 1970 under the pen of Michele Zecchini: former typesetter at *L'Humanité*, in charge of colonial affairs at the SFIO.

On your left, a vacuum cleaner sprawls below a garage door; a father pushes a stroller, single-handed, with a kid inside who will no doubt one day push another.

The date of his move to Paris still pesters historians and biographers: 1917, 1918, 1919. If the typesetter in question is to be believed—that is, assuming his memory is reliable so many years later, something neither you nor anyone else, for that matter, can swear to—the young Vietnamese man lived in the capital in July 1918, the month they met, and already had many friends. According to one Boris Souvarine, at the time a socialist activist, they had met there the year before.

But maybe none of this is important.

What may be important is that the world was about to come, or perhaps had just come, out of a war whose point we have yet to understand. Hunt down a dog, bash in a mule's nostrils, whip a horse, cram pigeons together—humans already applied themselves to such things; these were your species' daily bread. No doubt the aim here was to think bigger: to sew uniforms, line them as far as the eye could see and everywhere perforate them, to unroll barbed wire, wave flags with colored stripes, and take shells in the kisser or bullets in the flesh, like animals; a question of keeping busy. But Russia, kicking the tsar out and establishing here on earth a kingdom of less-than-nothings, had sanctioned a renewed belief, however small, in that proud letter standing on its two feet, the first of a funny word—Humanity, you mean.

Over there, on the other side of the Channel, Nguyên had earned his bread as an apprentice cook at the Carlton Hotel, but also as a snow shoveler, a bill poster, a garbageman, and a newsboy near Tube stations. He had played his part in strikes that shook the banks of the Thames, and was seen giving out food to the destitute, talking to Fabian Society reformists, and joining an obscure Annamite—or Vietnamese, let's say, since today it might as well be the same—clandestine organization. He had noticed that Whites sometimes killed other Whites, as in occupied Ireland, and had learned a word whose absence can compromise even life itself: revolution.

His date of birth is only safe to put forward in the plural. If we stick to the official date—as in, the one specified by the Party—he was twenty-eight in 1918. It's only arbitrarily that you also choose to use it: your motive is convenience.

This bedsit—a furnished room—no one can locate. There was a hotel at number 94 rue de Charonne, for unmarried men at that, but it closed in 1914. Nguyên lived alone, hidden,

5

his hands battered by frostbite and inflammation; there was nothing particularly charming about his isolation. It must be said that the native of Hoàng Trù, a village somewhere in the north of his country, had already spent two years at sea: aboard ships, freighters, liners, boats. All words for which the horizon is more than a straight line. On them he had learned how to handle spoons and forks, peel potatoes, polish kitchens, and serve the officers. Van Ba—his sobriquet as an odd-job man—thus came to know his fair share of ports of call around the wider world: here in Algeria, there in Lisbon, and again in Senegal, the Congo, Réunion, Egypt, Mexico, and Madagascar. He practiced his scrappy French with soldiers while bartering coffee for books, and had discovered, thanks to this trade, that there were decent Frenchmen, too. He had wandered down Marseille streets, under a heavy sun, ten sous in his pocket: tramways rolling by like so many houses on wheels, the misery of a conquering country, "Monsieur" they called him in Canebière bars—yes, him, really, the indigène.

And so here he is, after Boston and New York and Le Havre, after so many years spent as if spanning the pages of Cendrars or Istrati; here he is, the former engineman, street hawker, street sweeper, going in circles in a small bedroom on rue de Charonne.

One can still find pictures of this street from that time. You studied them to imagine the "proud and gaunt figure," as was said of him, "as thin as a shadow and always carrying a book," flanked by a horse carriage and kids in berets. You want to see him treading on cobblestones, and stick him awkwardly in there, this character, this cardboard cutout, makeshift and theatrical, beside the podgy woman or the carpenter. In *La*

Revue prolétarienne, the emigrant was depicted as small and frail—if quite tall for an Asian man, according to another source—his face emaciated, eyes at once soft and marked by fire. (That last detail you've had your fill of: his eyes—"sharp," "feverish," "brilliant," "blazing"—seem to have made quite an impression on those he crossed paths with.)

You give every appearance of searching for that lost, inconsequential room, but it is History, boisterously capitalized, that imposes itself on you as you make your way. There's the Charonne station, of course: where in 1962 nine protesters were murdered by the police and the admiring complicity of one Prime Minister Debré—beat up, bludgeoned, choked for wanting peace in Algeria. Farther away, number 92, you stop for a moment in front of the café La Belle Équipe, where, during a recent but already memorialized winter, two theocrats gunned down twice that number with .30 caliber rounds, cheering for God and Syria. One of them was the age Nguyên had been when he walked this same street in 1918. Even farther, at number 80, the memory takes shape—mingling smoke, blood, cobblestones, and Chassepots—of a barricade raised by the Commune against soldiers of the Republic, wretched Third of its name.

On a construction site, thick blue gloves stick out of a bag filled with sand and rubble; at nearby tables, customers sip sparkling water through their straws.

Nguyên moved out.

We don't know the street, only that it is located, should we keep listening to the typesetter, on the left bank of the Seine, somewhere within the 13th arrondissement's seven square kilometers. Cramped lodgings shared with a Tunisian man by the name of Moktar, an anticolonial militant who worked at an ordnance factory.

Nguyên's documents weren't in order; he steered clear of neighbors, hiding between his four walls for fear of running into law enforcement. These first few weeks, he wouldn't turn on the light or touch the stove in the absence of his comrade, who, upon his return from drudgery, would prepare Nguyên's meals for the next day. The apartment was humid, walls wept, wind blew between doors and windows. The typesetter would stop by and read the day's headlines to him; they played cards, then drank wine when night fell—white? red? no matter—until the Tunisian returned.

Nguyên Tât Thanh's face was gaunt, his complexion sallow, his eyes literally jumped out at you—or so the typesetter would record many years later. Again those eyes. Unusual mettle. The ascetic's bewitching fervor. His interlocutor would recall telling himself that this stray of a man was destined to go far.

The SFIO—which Nguyên joined at the end of 1918, or maybe at the start of the following year, none can agree—had verified his identity and was committed to providing him with documents. One of its members, by the name of Paul Vaillant-Couturier, had in fact tasked our typesetter with assisting the young emigrant. Vaillant-Couturier wasn't even thirty years old; a bit of a poet, a bit of a painter, in the fighting he'd been injured twice, with shrapnel in his hip as an infantryman, and then aboard a tank, with poison gas. The war left him without these Heavens to which he tried to hang on, still, so as not to grab life as it unfortunately is, crude, all too coarse; up there, there's only nitrogen, argon, neon, or methane—no need to throw more. A pacifist, Vaillant-Couturier at the time wrote for the pages of the satirical *Canard enchaîné*; he was soon to become a socialist deputy in parliament, then a communist militant, and would feature, half-turning aside, with his dark, supple hair, next to a Nguyên in black tie and white collar, in one of the rare pictures of him taken during this period.

But the Annamite would soon leave this makeshift home.

A PMU, an African restaurant, secondhand and record stores (jazz, Caribbean, funk), a health promotion center (which you remember visiting some time ago) and posters on streetlamps for some candidate or other, three "agents for urban cleanliness," four men bent over sewing machines in a fabric shop (wax, bazin, java), a grocery (plantains, fried cod, cassava leaves) and a shopping cart padlocked to a sidewalk barrier, a picture of Lili Brik (you remember Mayakovsky's bedroom, of course: her lover of a poet who, you can't recall the exact date, sent a bullet through his own heart, apartment 12, his farewell letter linking everyday life to the image of a small, smashed boat; you'd seen it a long time ago: it snowed upon Moscow's rooftops and the wreckage of your love) and then a placard resting against a tree, on which one can read, in purple ink: Animals Deserve To Live Free & Not Exploited.

You go up rue Marcadet, two kilometers long, heart of the 18th arrondissement—the capital's north, a good hour's walk from Charonne. Ten or so documents in four different languages attest to his next lodging: a bedsit, a cubbyhole, a poorly furnished room. If none of them can help find its exact address, or even agree on the exact year of his move, two at least prove to be somewhat precise; one dates from the end of the 1960s, the other from the early 1990s. Nguyên lived "within sight" or "not far" from the Marcadet metro station, known today as Marcadet-Poissonniers, boasting five access points shared among three major thoroughfares . . . In his time, the two names were separate, and the Marcadet metro entrances were located on boulevard Barbès. Everything leads you to believe that Nguyên's room was in the first third of the street you're now pacing. This bedsitter he shared with Annamite anarchists, or so claims a source, then president of the ORTF.

Idle and lively people, onlookers and hands compelled into hurry by wage-labor; two thirtysomethings jog and a restaurant sign flickers; wheels toing and froing; the city growls, fawn gray, while the gutter scoffs down water. The metro opens its big mouth—you wouldn't be against seeing some of Giono's wild boars emerge from it, the dream of a Paris pulverized by sprouting trees. A man walks, beanie dragged over his skull, struggling with the weight of his life and of his suitcase; another carries an ancient armchair on his shoulders, legs to the sky, alongside someone who seems to be his partner. This specter you're chasing around follows that of Rodin, half a century later: the artist had settled in the area next to a certain Rose, a working woman he swore was as beautiful as a statue.

About halfway up, silence falls suddenly and a molting takes place: the popular street adjusts its clothes and, just like the seated child you see through a barbershop window, has its nape swept by a shaving brush. Balsamic vinegar glaze snakes its way down white plates; here, the passerby can acquire "vintage" decorative objects, as well as "artisanal" cheeses and furniture. You make a stop at 129, at which address Alain Geismar, then a militant in the Proletarian Left, paid tribute to Maoist worker Pierre Overney, felled, some three years after the death of Hô Chi Minh, by a security officer at the Renault company; the murderer would be bumped off five years later by the Armed Nuclei for Popular Autonomy, while the militant eventually returned to a more conventional life. A woman in formless gray is at a standstill, on the phone, while another passes by, wrapped in a scarf the same orange as her shopping cart. A small truck is waiting, engine on in the chilly air, and you think, God knows why, of a description sketched out by one of Hô Chi Minh's biographers, and based on a Parisian picture of Nguyên Tât Thanh—extremely rare, as you said before: the young man wore a bowler hat and had an expression not unlike that of the Little Tramp in *The Immigrant* or *The Pilgrim*. He seemed "lost," "broken"; he didn't have the grotesque look of the sentences you underlined in a Party publication, put out by Hanoi Editions: Marx's heir, a "genius" whose work will establish "Spring eternal."

Hang on.

It's that you quite like this picture. You don't know much about the Tramp, meaning, like everyone else, a few famous images, something vague about world heritage, a vagrant and his toothbrush mustache. But there's more to say. For one, there's that fresco on a wall in Dreux you passed by at random: an unhappy Tramp sitting, arms crossed, next to a small white dog with a black left eye. You stopped in your tracks and took a photo. And then there's *Ulysses*, by Fondane. Long, flowing poems you gladly make your own, these verses unbridled by rhyme, the soul of harbors; you were always going to like that text. You read it multiple times, in two versions, one of which was published in Belgium in 1933, the other in 1944, the year of his demise at Auschwitz. In its words, from part nine: "Later, when I saw Chaplin I understood those emigrants, / later, much later myself . . . / [. . .] I ask no more for the meaning of the world / I pound my fist on the table of the world." Thus a dog and his human brother, thus a poet. You know it doesn't make much sense, but you like the image. Doubtless, the unruly poet and the rough sleeper in a frock coat from *A Dog's Life* are suddenly linked, overlaid by an author's imagination and then your own. Maybe this is how rectitude and tenderness meet, a dubious compound that struggles, we know, to impart the true measure of revolutions. But here these two things are mixed with others you knew nothing about, catching up to your daydream. First, there's this meeting that no one seems in a position to confirm: Nguyen Tât Thanh may have made the great actor's acquaintance on the high seas, some time prior to his arrival in Paris—and so according to an account by Chaplin's daughter published in the Cuban press. The Vietnamese man asked for his autograph, aboard a ship of some sort, before they shared a conversation in the kitchens. And then there's this veteran of the Battle of Alsace acquainted with him, who noted that he had "something Chaplinesque about him," something sad and comical at the same time. And also this sentence unearthed in a copious English-language biography: in 1946, then newly elected president Hô Chi Minh revealed to a reporter, in front of a crowd gathered for his visit to the Champs-Élysées, that he thought it quite normal that everyone would want to see—in your translation—"a Vietnamese version of Charlie Chaplin." And so the cold-blooded insurgent and the funny-looking fellow, leader despite himself brandishing the flag of *Modern Times*, have full leave to stroll, together, the very street you're walking on . . .

A bistro and a tent appear at the next intersection, the latter housing three homeless people; farther on, the same number of men, work uniforms speckled with mud, are cleaning the road with water jets and brooms, a few paces from a "sustainable" kitchen supplies shop. An "Abolition de la société de classe" poster, half-torn, colors one of the nearby walls: Paris seems a hundred years older and yet, more than ever, those words wait for their time. You pass by a home for young working women (now mixed-sex), a hypno-therapist and "life coach" practice, and a mother asking her son whether he plans on taking his violin. Four adolescents are singing, their football kicked on ahead of them along the sidewalk; a garbage bin spits out leaves; a jeweler offers "chic and natural" items that, of course, "defy trends"; a graffiti, partly covered, exclaims joyfully, We Don't Know It Yet But We Are Anarchists!

Rue Marcadet ends here, at Guy-Môquet station. Of the rebel with the round hat and burning eyes who apparently read Dickens, Tolstoy, and Romain Rolland, nothing but air.

You order a coffee at the bar in front of you; sugar; take a pocket-sized book of Lebanese photography out of your parka, recently given by a friend with whom you traveled Vietnam from south to north; leaf through it. Punctured facades, dented cars, automatic rifles, thick smoke, the rubble of a brothel—"An end-of-the-world atmosphere reigned in this abandoned city."

On June 18, 1919, Nguyên Tât Thanh disappeared forever: he vanished into a collective, the Groupe des patriotes annamites—nicknamed the Five Dragons—members of which borrowed the alias Nguyên Ai Quâc before that name became his only. Then the letter *a* would lose the horns that mark its distant, oxen origins, rounding into an eyelike *o*: Ai Quôc, which is how the future Hô Chi Minh would be known until 1942: the Patriot, he who loves his country.

His signature is found at the bottom of a text written as negotiations were opening in Versailles to finalize the treaty of that name and thereby conclude four years of world war. That is, conclude it with a document laid out in so many pages, in parts and articles, in sections a, b, and c, in subsections and appendixes, in billions of marks and tons of coal, in coal tar and foals, in dairy cows and customs duties—for such clutter to be contained in print, dozens of commissions had to be mobilized, thousands of meetings, and who knows how many diplomats, delegations, and experts.

On one side, the victors; on the other, the Reich, finally defeated. One year earlier, President Wilson had delivered a speech in fourteen points to promote peace, free trade, and the sovereignty of nations. Nguyên had taken careful note of the fifth, precisely that which some North American secretary of state, "convinced of the danger of putting such an idea in the mind of certain races," hadn't appreciated; this was the point that made mention of colonial territories and "the interests of the populations concerned." The Dragons' appeal was titled "Demands of the Annamite People": it was directed at the Entente's most powerful members; it spoke very highly, in forceful capital letters, of the Noble French People and their sublime ideal of universal fraternity; it suggested that the French would be doing their duty toward France and Humanity if they took heed of the oppressed; it hoped for eight concrete reforms. That is: amnesty for indigène political prisoners, an end to the dual legal system, freedom of speech and of the press, freedom of association, academic and educational freedoms, and the replacement of rule by decree by rule of law, as well as the establishment in French parliament of a permanent delegation of indigènes.

A most restrained tone.

Barely a tickle, soft nothings. No onset of secession, no foretaste of revolution, no hint of rifles cracking beneath the moon — not even a peashooter. The first liberal in sight would've gladly co-signed it. Trouble is, none of its authors had Mr. Wilson's height, Mr. Lloyd George's blue irises, Mr. Clemenceau's pale complexion, or Mr. Orlando's pointy nose, these four being the members of the Council for Peace. And that spoiled everything. The Republic, Human Rights:

so many amusing finds. The King had been shortened by about a tenth of his height, God told to ratchet down, and powdered wigs stuffed down the trunks of carriages on the run—yet with no hint of contradiction, workers, the under-class and the ill-to-do were still bludgeoned, troops or law enforcement still sent to put a few down every once in a while, a reminder that universal suffrage is never so prized as in good society; sometimes even a few thousand were put down at once on the capital's cobblestones, and Messrs. Flaubert and Zola could congratulate themselves that order was restored; then it started all over again, seats at the National Assembly, polls, governments, cabinets, the great national debates: they should eventually be made to quiet down, those, there, with only their hands to live by, red heaps, black rags, the Nation's stiff necks, who knows, someday soon they'll even be offered the very cars they're producing. One might even invite them to kill each other on the country's borders, or on the side of the world where noses don't point, where irises shine black: master and miserable finally united under a single banner! Bright idea! The ungrateful should be locked up or done away with for good: one does not balk at democracy.

And so, on that June 18, 1919, Nguyên went to Versailles to submit the Dragons' appeal, relayed that morning in the third page of *L'Humanité* and written, for the most part, by two of his comrades already known to the police: he would explain, as Hô Chi Minh, that his command of French wasn't all that good. Of this visit, we don't have much to add except that, as specified in a report drafted by the French Central Intelligence Service and the Sûreté, it didn't succeed.

According to one of his biographers, he was even ushered out "unceremoniously."

Admittedly, more than half a million of the French Empire's indigènes had gone to war for the motherland; admittedly, about one hundred thousand Indochinese had come to fight or work for the motherland; admittedly, the treaty these gentlemen labored assiduously upon was about to strip Germany of its colonies—the French Empire would help itself to large plots of Cameroon and Togo; the British Empire would make off with Tanganyika, Southwest Africa, New Guinea, Nauru, and Samoa; the Belgian Empire would pocket Ruanda-Urundi (Japan would have to content itself with islands). Admittedly. But these gentlemen had more important things to discuss than a twenty-nine-year-old knockabout.

This is how the state is made: deaf as a doornail. A big iron doornail. One may formulate two or three reasonable demands, resolutely decent, even bowing slightly, eyelids lowered, and see it gloat in return from the commanding heights occupied by its fat iron ass. One may swear that one's had enough, really enough; it'll invoke the law that it, lucky coincidence, designed. At this juncture, one may knock down a ministry door, or sketch thick clusters of smoke in the sky by burning the cars, apartments, or restaurants of its most well-to-do citizens, and all of a sudden, it sees you. Should one turn a police station or van into ashes, then one will be let inside—for torture, first, then negotiations. It's grim, but this is how the state is made.

Maybe Versailles hadn't looked hard enough into Nguyên's eyes.

As for the press, it didn't say a word.

You have a look at the next day's issues—columns in the *Figaro*, the *Petit journal*, the *Matin*, the *Petit Parisien*, *La Croix*: nothing doing. And so, he would soon go to Moscow, to Crimea, to Hong Kong; he would be declared dead, cruise the oceans, end up in prison, write poems, and call on poets to coat their verses in steel. And then he would discuss, compose, negotiate, state that blood is only misery; reply that war will break out for a hundred years if the French state continues to ignore us, and then arrive, soft-spoken, at a resolution: let's fight. Then he would raise an army whose black sandals are carved out of tire rubber, and he would smash the Empire.

Ingratitude doesn't number among the virtues. Let's therefore praise the police: lending a hand to historians. The force's passion for surveillance, espionage, tracking, notes, tails, reports, informers, and dirty tricks ensures the delight of future audiences, and yours with them. In Aix-en-Provence, the National Archives for Overseas France keeps the file "Nguyen Ai Quôc," compiled by an agent named Paul Arnoux, in the form of a belt-strapped canvas folder.

On the first page, reverse side: his "report," enlivened by a picture taken on the sly on pont Alexandre III (the man in question is smoking, brows furrowed, bowler hat); he is described in every physical detail (the shape of his forehead, the tone of his skin, the volume of his nostrils, the positioning of his ears). A graceless figure emerges from these lines:

his appearance is "gauche," he stoops a little, his smile is somewhat "witless."

The French embassy had requested as early as June 1915 that British authorities monitor him because of the company he kept, yet the first mention of him in Paris refers to June 6, 1919: the young man had just left London and stayed for four days at 10 rue de Stockholm, in the 8th arrondissement, then at 56 rue Monsieur-le-Prince, from June 12 to July 13, in the 6th. According to this confidential document, addressed to the governor-general of Indochina, Nguyên didn't step foot on French soil during the war. Hence: confusion on the part of the witnesses swearing they rubbed shoulders with him in the years prior, or oversight on the part of the intelligence services? We know, in any case, that a certain president of the republic, by the name of Poincaré, was personally preoccupied with the troublemaker.

Four metro stations, about fifteen minutes.

The Gare Saint-Lazare's rooftops reveal their serrated shape from the end of a narrow street. The blue that crowns it seems marked with off-white diagonal scratches; cobblestones suffocate, wholly drowned in shade; wherever your eyes fall, not a soul in sight—the presence of a passerby wouldn't change a thing. At the aforementioned number 10, a three-star hotel bears the name of an American president: a hundred to two hundred euros a night, massages on demand and air conditioning. Three potted box-tree balls decorate the putty-gray facade; light only shines on about half the edifice. This establishment was apparently built in 1900; its "guest relations manager" will tell you that management can offer absolutely no information to help your case.

You go to the train station facing you (the same you saw gassed, recently, as you came and went, part of this faceless you that makes the beauty of a crowd suddenly formed, amid the shards of tear gas grenades, the high-vis gillets jaunes of the uncounted, and the shots of short-ranged projectiles).

On a map of Paris—one-twenty-thousandth scale—you marked with colored dots all the places for which there are hints, or evidence, of his visit. If the capital keeps quiet about him, mute under your steps, you at least have this: a curious constellation on the flatness of paper.

Two metro lines, a second hotel with the same star count, lodged between a Vietnamese restaurant and a hairdresser. It's therefore here, a few strides from the Jardin du Luxembourg, that Nguyên spent one summer month. Amber lighting, pale facade, planters on cast-iron balconies. The call from the Groupe des patriotes annamites had been addressed to the French press, as well as to all the representatives from the countries gathered for the Treaty of Versailles; twelve thousand copies were then distributed to militants of the SFIO, to the CGT, as well as to the Human Rights League. Here is the address, 56 rue Monsieur-le-Prince, that Nguyên wrote at the bottom of a letter sent to the American secretary of state to apprise him of the Annamites' eight points. Silence from the bicycles standing in line, the street as if holding its breath.

In his *City Poetics*, Pierre Sansot makes mention of a "topology of the outskirts": great urban areas "spill over their own limits"; these spaces spread, monopolize their environs.

Streets and facades speak, he goes on, witnesses to the "individual and collective history of peoples": the city thus becomes the "unsurmountable horizon of our promises." Brook or pavement, forest or ring road, your heart isn't in the bargain; you nonetheless know that if walls suffocate the earth, these, even collapsed, keep our old dreams upright.

Rimbaud lived a hundred meters further on, at number 41, the Orient Hotel—Stella, today. He wasn't yet eighteen and, in a letter to a childhood friend mailed a year after the crushing of the Commune, admitted: "I smoked my hammer pipe and spat on rooftop tiles, because it was an attic." At number 20, Malik Ossekine, only a few years older than the poet, was felled a century later by the batons of Charles Pasqua's Interior Ministry, after leaving a jazz concert. (While the people, in garments of shrill yellow, now rise up for a better life and see, in return, their eyes gouged out and their hands torn off, a member of parliament for the majority party, all progressive that he is, swears, as you're writing these very pages, that this corpse is better left forgotten.) Under your eyes, and you use this preposition in the strictest sense since you indeed need to lower them, a plaque in his memory: bright capital letters over muted charcoal gray.

The street comes to an end at an exploded bouquet of yellow roses, their petals scattered on the asphalt below a garbage can; a Chanel handbag; and a wall urging you to join the rebellion—an anonymous hand, no doubt painted under the cover of darkness, and a great green hourglass, nowadays the international symbol for the fight against the extinction of species and climate change. The most ambitious of our forebears, you think, saw in the future the remedy to cure the world's ills; their offspring are doing the utmost to save what they can of it.

The streets lead you at their whim to boulevard Saint-Germain.

On July 13, Nguyên the Patriot moved to the Croulebarbe neighborhood, at number 6 villa des Gobelins. That morning, the *Petit Journal* offered revenge to the motherland: on the front page, defeated Germany was styled as a crestfallen woman, spiked helmet atop her blonde hair and weapon broken at her feet, facing an erect Marianne, imperious and commanding, dazzling red Phrygian cap and sword planted upright.

Under a striped umbrella and on the avenue that shares a name with the villa in question, amid the fragmented shadows of ash trees and Chinese cedars, a shoe shiner is on the lookout for clients. Colorful rags, little metal pots, polishing brushes, and overlong pants, rolled up. You walk past a factory that was transformed into an arms and munitions depot during the Commune, before being torched, though only partly, to thwart the soldiery.

The street has a very Haussmanian rigidity. Between a restaurant and an estate agent, on your right, this "villa," which means dead end. Something like seventy meters. Gray silence. Nothing hanging from the balconies. You would like to be describing a bird's flight, but there are only plants in a wooden tray. The building is four stories high; its bricks are painted yellow; a plaque indicates, near the entrance, the presence of a pediatrician and a general practitioner.

You give the door a push, who knows; closed, without question. You could come back another day, and maybe you will, fully aware, nonetheless, that the medical community will be of no assistance. The Marxist lawyer Phan Van Truong rented an apartment here—on the second floor, you read in a note addressed to Paris's prefect of police from the office of the governor-general of Indochina—and lodged a number of his comrades, including Nguyên. High forehead, full face, thick mustache, this man, then in his lower forties, was thought by the French police to be the soul of the Groupe des patriotes annamites. Incarcerated in a military prison in 1914—then again the following decade—and admitted to the Paris bar three years later, Phan helped Nguyên write his articles, even if that meant he reworked them more than their author would've liked. He died in 1933, largely forgotten, as Nguyên, at the time leader of the Indochinese Communist Party, fled through China after his arrest by the British police (who threw him in solitary under a false identity and declared him dead), before running to Vladivostok, 43rd parallel north.

But in this year 1919, Nguyên was only about to donate five francs to *L'Humanité* to put up a monument in honor of Jean Jaurès, felled five years earlier, a Smith & Wesson bullet in the head for refusing to believe that opening Europe's belly to dump its children in, that was a fate worth fighting for.

There still exists an identity card bearing the name Nguyên Ai Quôc, dated September 4, 1919. Residing: villa des

Gobelins. Profession: student. Height: 1.65 meters (three centimeters taller than in his police file); eyes: black; distinguishing marks: none; nose: flat bridge, horizontal base, sizeable; skin tone: olive. A blue or purple stamp, the police chief's initials, two signatures. In the customary photo, Nguyên sports an impeccable round collar, three-piece suit, dark tie, and pulled-back hair. He is smooth-chinned, his head at a slight angle. Not quite looking into the camera. The Party swore that he was born in 1890; this proof of identity takes four years off him—of no consequence: the state reveals all except what truly matters.

Two days after the card was issued, the young man was received by Albert Sarraut, a Radical-Socialist member of parliament. You don't know where—his office or his home, probably. No doubt a few words are in order. Former governor-general of French Indochina and future minister, in turn, of the Colonies, the Navy, the Interior and Education, Sarraut would go on to publish a book entitled *Bringing the French Colonies to the Fore* and vote to grant full powers to Pétain seventeen years later. Though the leader of the long Vietnamese resistance, De Thám, had been executed on his orders on the eve of the Great War—two blows (pickaxe), his head cut off and displayed in a market, flies and all for onlookers—the elected official wasn't a complete nutjob. Certainly no raving zealot, drool hanging from his lips: just the well-heeled voice of reform and of the Colonial Party.

We don't know what they talked about; however, we do know that Nguyên wrote to him as early as the next day to send a copy of the Dragons' demands, assuring him of his respect, urging him to implement them.

We know, also, that he went to the Parisian residence of Jules Cambon, then general secretary at the Foreign Affairs ministry—his niece, Geneviève Tabouis, would relate this story in *The Princes of Peace*. Nguyên Ai Quôc had wished to show him their eight-point program so that this former governor of Algeria could pass it to Clemenceau, to whom he was close: Cambon refused to talk to the young man. In 1980, the niece revealed that her uncle was far too busy and that the courteous Annamite boasted eyes that matched the descriptions cited earlier. She wouldn't hear about him again until she met him a second time, a few months before the Indochina War broke out—twenty-seven years later, in other words; he had, in the meantime, swapped suit and tie for tunic and sandals.

You imagine him then, this slender if stout-hearted body, knocking on the doors of your country's greats during the day to plead for a cause all considered lost, and, come nightfall, warming his bed with a hot brick wrapped in old newspapers; you wonder what he felt, this man, whose mother spun silk and whose father, a tippler and quick to anger, had been dismissed from his position as magistrate several months before Nguyên took to the sea aboard a six-thousand-ton steamer, doing so without breathing a word of it to his family: abandoning all for the waters, kitchen hand that he was, for halting conversations, for a smoke in the mouth, to ignite furnaces and carry coal—what he must've felt in the face of the rejections, presumably polite, that he suffered. "Black, thin, famished devil / Riddled with scabs and bruises / Just as well / Patient I am—unwavering," would write the Patriot in the darkness of his cell many years later. Maybe patience was an old habit. Nguyên was nonetheless disappointed, they say, with the silence that answered their program.

You try your hardest not to read his story topsy-turvy, that is, on the strength of an ending known to all. This "success story," crude, as all of them are, is always around the corner. An effective narrative: from destitute to war chief, from nobody to stone-carved hero with a child in his arms. These rejections, these failures, you wish not to grasp in the light of his future victory, not to see these debacles as preludes to his consecration, as an unwound thread that no obstacle can sever. If one *enters* History, there must be a threshold to cross: a definitive border between two conditions, between those who die and those whom death doesn't kill. What's certain, for now, is that this young man doesn't have the future all to himself yet; Nguyên has his faith and his good fortune: no car ran him over as he left the ministry man's home.

With every page you turn in his file, handwritten or typed, the extent of the surveillance to which Nguyên was subjected comes to light. His mail was inspected, his comings and goings noted down to the minute, the papers he bought indexed, the visitors he received listed, the metros he took logged. Grocery shopping and visits to the cleaner's, nothing was missing. The names of several agents come up repeatedly: two in particular, at the start, Édouard and Jean. The first, you read, spoke the Annamite language; the second is the alias of warrant officer Lâm: two indigènes in service of the Empire.

Notes from one of them sketch the portrait of an intelligent young man, likely from the north of Annam, who resorted to using the pseudonym Ho Ba and admits co-authoring the Five Dragons' call. Those of his colleague reveal the mission's daily requirements: we learn, for the end of 1919 alone, that the spy: judged "Nguyên Ai Quâc" to be only the cover name of a collective, but had not yet found out where the young man was from, nor anything about his family (November 3); paid Nguyên a visit pretending to be a merchant keen to work with Indochina (December 1); interrogated his building's concierge (December 8); took the militant to be a well-educated man, who knew how to read and write in French, English, Spanish, and even a little Italian, and who spent his days studying and reading, and intended to stay in France so as to freely express himself on the situation in Indochina (December 10); asked him to translate a Chinese advertisement so as to find out whether he had mastered that language (December 15); thought that Quôc, as he called him, was so absorbed in his studies that he harbored a dislike for the female sex (December 18); and learned from Nguyên's own mouth that he'd never been to Japan or China (December 29).

This Jean had managed to win Nguyên's trust to the extent that the latter advised him to be careful when he came by villa des Gobelins. "We are being watched," he'd even told him. In October, the militant had asked Jean to sign his letters with the first name Jeannette, and admitted to registering for English classes at the Sorbonne, on Tuesdays and Fridays, as a cover.

A summary adds that Nguyên wrote autonomist leaflets, carefully concealed his true identity, spent his days at the National Library (an hour's walk from the villa, you find) and the Sainte-Geneviève Library (twenty-five minutes, Left Bank), went to the offices of the Human Rights League, and kept the company of "questionable peers." The document relates again that the militants' conversations, in their homes, were likely to drag on until one in the morning, and so not without making noise, and that the Dragons were now known to nearly all Annamite groups. Then it concludes: agents were constantly in contact with the man in question, and one of them—Jean, you guess—wouldn't be long, close to him as he was now, in uncovering the mystery of his identity.

On behalf of a Chinese newspaper called *Yi Che Pao*, an American correspondent interviewed Nguyên Ai Quôc in the middle of September 1919.

While it remains difficult to know which of the five Dragons was hiding behind the various publications bearing the signature Nguyên Ai Quôc or any of its orthographic variants—since we know that the pen could still be held, at that time, by any one of them—the description that introduces this interview leaves little room for doubt as to the person of flesh and blood met by the journalist: he was the one the world would remember by the name Hô Chi Minh.

To a question about his reasons for coming to France, the militant responded that he intended to demand the freedoms due to his people. To one about his program, he responded, "Move ever forward in accordance with our strengths." Then he let it be known that his only hope, in this country, lay in the support of socialists.

A copy landed, as you might expect, on the desk of the Central Intelligence Service.

Tuesday, the following month.

The French Senate had just ratified the Treaty of Versailles and, on the other side of the Rhine, a certain Adolf Hitler, thirty years old, as yet unknown to all, son of a former domestic servant and a customs inspector passionate about bees, would in five days join the new German Workers' Party, future vehicle for Nazism. These were times, he would remember in *Mein Kampf*, of creation, left and right, of new organizations, such was the citizenry's total lack of trust in the already existing parties. That Tuesday, October 14, 1919, the socialist daily *Le Populaire*, headed by Marx's grandson — Longuet was his name — published an open letter by "Nguyèn-ai-Quâc."

One could read, on its front page, about the forces of law and order clobbering workers in Brest with their truncheons, or about the mechanics on strike in Marseille successfully hindering two liners attempting to leave the dock. On the second page, advertisements for perfume and shoe polish, and a few excerpts from the letter in question. Its addressee? Deputy Ernest Outrey.

Posterity has shunned the name. One might recall for a moment his quarrels with the young Malraux, but only for a moment, before ambling away, whistling. What else is there to say? That his parents first saw the light of day on land that none yet called Iraq or Turkey; that he had sworn to be faithful to some lady five years before in

Saigon, one day Hô Chi Minh City, and had worked as a civil servant in Laos and Cambodia; that he had the luxury of being able to decorate his suits, of which you could swear to the neatness of every fold, with the five starry arms of the Légion d'honneur; that he had published two or three things the need for which was questionable, such as his *New Compendium of Annamite Canton and Commune Legislation in Cochinchina*, and that he wore a monocle and a large, somewhat silly mustache, trimmed with care. He also represented, you're getting to it, the south of modern-day Vietnam at the Chamber of Deputies of the Third Republic, and sat on the bench with the Radicals' parliamentary group—a coterie of liberals, centrists, and humanists partial to private property.

To take possession of a land and redden it with the blood of its inhabitants, one needs more than gunpowder and the edge of a blade: Civilization, Freedom, and outpourings of pretty penmanship regarding infrastructure, divine spirit, and progress make for solid points of reference. But to you, Outrey appears to be a man for the concrete, of a type that cherishes pragmatism as others do virtue, one plus one and cold hard cash: "All of our current colonial policy [is] conditioned by the question of raw materials," he would write in the pages of the *Monde illustré*. Good intentions, break formation! It's just that cotton proved to be essential to the textile industry in the northern and eastern parts of the metropole, and that Indochinese silk had to supply Lyon's factories after the closure of the Chinese market.

Nguyên's recent statements in the pages of the *Populaire* hadn't been to Outrey's liking—one must say that Nguyên's style had lost some of its roundaboutness: in the name of peace on all five continents, it was now a matter of exterminating the imperialist hydra wherever the people of the world met it. The emigrant assailed the "monster," the "foreign yoke" and the "brainwashing" that prevailed over there, in his home, and mentioned his compatriots who, by the tens of thousands, would never again see their native country. Outrey proved to be so displeased that he opened by opining on it at the National Assembly, ranting at once against this hateful wretch, this enemy of France and of the peace that reigns in "happy" Indochina.

Nguyên Ai Quôc would insult him in return and insisted on pointing out that his protest was addressed to bad Frenchmen, not to France.

One report explains that our group of Asian activists suffered from bronchitis and tuberculosis, and that the small-mindedness of their enterprise wasn't likely to make an impression in Indochina (though enough of an impression, apparently, for their spokesman to be mentioned in parliament). Another report describes Nguyên's dismal lifestyle: bread, milk, the occasional sausage. The man, it reads, tried to take the floor during a socialist meeting: negative. Smiles at the clumsiness of the one they sometimes called "the Montmartre mute."

Nguyên, who stammered the moment he stepped forward in public, went to Socialist Party meetings, to the Bourse du travail, and to the CGT; to the theater, the museum, the library; he considered means of spreading images of his country in cinemas so that the French might get acquainted with it.

As for the authorities, they lost themselves in guesswork regarding his identity: Wasn't his name Antoine, by the way? But one day in February, the young man successfully delivered a speech. He spoke of his people, enslaved, dazed by alcohol and opium, of mistreated women, and of the French capitalists who enriched themselves on their backs. For the first time, yes, he spoke openly.

A crinkled Moleskine notebook—your old notes from Vietnam. It was lying around, more or less forgotten, in a crate with similar-looking objects. You turn the pages, images come to mind that your memory is more than willing to color in again, others that you shut up, sometimes abruptly, and that memory attempts in vain to revive. Here, a pier, the Mekong river battered by rain, and a boat hoisting a red, starred flag; there, a child slides a small snake into one of his nostrils. There, a hike, a backpack, fish jumping out of the water, a dense forest, the mauve froth of the morning sky; there, conversations with an old guerrilla fighter. Here, you lie at the edge of your hut while your companion sleeps in the shade; there, you talk to an old poet fond of French writers, some of whom you're unfamiliar with (starting with Proust). Words pass by, as do the kilometers: faces, lights, pigments, streets, signs, rice paddies, trains, fruits, bars, animals, books (so this is where you read Che's *Bolivian Diary*). These pages are of no use here. Except that a name comes up again and again in some of them, one that belongs to the author of a poetry collection purchased around then, *Prison Diary*, signed Hô Chi Minh two decades after he left Paris.

"We will try to work miracles," Lenin stated, jaw clenched. But the year 1920, then marking its first days in chalk on Russian walls, was a sorry spectacle. The civil war dragged on; the Red Army had just wrested control of a city none yet called Stalingrad from a White general; famine and flu blighted Moscow. Workers grumbled in their factories. And Lenin articulated the need for an additional war against hunger, cold, and deterioration. And Trotsky, busy supervising transports, swore that the policy of complete centralization and nationalization couldn't carry on in this way—what he didn't swear, the People's Commissar dictated in notes that would soon become the book *Terrorism and Communism*: a way of answering their critics, the big mud-slinging mouths and that of Kautsky in particular, damned German who, proud Marxist that he claimed to be, hadn't words harsh enough for Bolshevism. Trotsky threw himself at this with the language that you know well, knife-like, steel, straight to the heart; he stuck to it and accepted, never with a blink, never with a frown, never with anything that might give even the impression of a quiver, that, yes, to destroy the rotten system of exploitation, it takes iron and blood and terror, that, yes, when the enemy's armies are out to get you, the only thing left is to shoot the capitalists and shut down the press in their pay.

But about that, detractors and mud-slingers, Nguyên Ai Quôc was all at sea. The fuss made about the revisionism

33

of some and the leftism of others, the excerpts from Marx thrown like insults in so many faces and the Engels exegeses invoked to the rescue; all that, at sea.

He couldn't grasp, at first, these words that resonated again and again at every meeting and in his ears: reformism, anarchism, utopian socialism, collectivism, thesis, antithesis. Those he looked out for, regretting their absence, would've sounded more like colonies, empire, liberation. He couldn't understand the reasons driving these men to tear each other apart over ideas while others lost their lives. And when he borrowed *Capital* from a library in the 13th arrondissement, near the Place d'Italie, the big book served as his pillow.

That was because the urgent need, Nguyên confided in agent Lâm, alias Jean, in this the early part of 1920, was to be loud and clear. Loud everywhere so that it be known—far from the racket of the soldiers of the Revolution and of the last tsarists, pouring their guts out on the snow—what had been afoot in Indochina ever since cross-wielders, cannoneers, and merchants began to take it for their precious little jewel of the Orient. "Jail me, exile me, cut my head off, it doesn't matter," he confided again to the agent, who told the authorities, who then filed it in their good books—those same books you're consulting today. To be loud and to write. No doubt it was the same. Nguyên therefore passed his time at the library, reading books so as to write his own. Four chapters, recounting the history of Indochina, from its subjugation to its necessary liberation. Jean asked him how he expected to finance its publication; Nguyên responded that he would pay a visit to a socialist militant and offer to work for him—as a servant, shoe shiner, handyman, didn't matter. He hoped to be able to finish it in two months, and thought about calling it *The Oppressed*; criticism would be forthcoming regarding the violence of such a title; he answered that he didn't fear the courts; better, he would use them as his podium.

A walk is work for feet, but even more for digression. Hints of ideas jump out only to end in puddles, sentences escape the hands of streets, words bounce off the cobblestones, memories start up without so much as announcing themselves. Walking, or writing with your eyes closed.

In the distance, plane-traced vapor trails behind the Panthéon's triple dome. The cutlery of outdoor diners clinks; rumblings, humming, the noises of a city muffled as if stuffed inside a burlap sack. A church advertises a Chopin concert mere steps from a Chevy Corvette at a standstill; a revolutionary poster is clashing.

You get to the Place du Panthéon. A group of students are in conversation, seated in a shadow cast by the monument (you wouldn't mind a conversation with Rousseau's remains); between two columns of the nearby town hall, a little breeze makes wrinkles of the flag's three colors; the motto of the republic—Liberté Égalité Fraternité—sits atop a university entrance (Hô Chi Minh said that it piqued his interest as a teenager: how, in short, could the pleasant maxim of Desmoulins, Forty-Eighters, and Communards end up in the buttonholes of grandees and infantrymen? Seems to you as if benefits could be derived from asking it every morning, that question.)

A scooter overtakes you (an exotic maneuver for the provincial that you are); couples pose, twisted mouths, outstretched arms, eyes inspired for the favors of a selfie (perhaps an offering to our "brothers in the order of the Night," from bloody Malraux, buried there, just behind them?); you draw near the Sainte-Geneviève Library. Inside, two million documents; outside, young people having a snack. In one of his novels, Jules Vallès relates that he went inside hoping to hear sounds of outrage; a flop: "Not a single angry mug in the whole lot!" As for you, it was with the intention, less daring, to make copies of Algerian poems, otherwise impossible to find, that you went in one day.

Idler, you won't be venturing inside again: your memories are enough for this walk: a reading room like a basilica nave or the bridge of a five-masted ship, pierced by white light from so many windows (forty-one, after checking); half-moon lamps and long rows of glossy wood tables; books everywhere caught in a web of wood and iron. Need only sketch Nguyên's silhouette from among them, "as frail as a swallow but [. . .] consumed by a crusader's fire," and then add to these words lifted from a libertarian largely forgotten of pointed quills: large cheekbones and a large mouth, hollow cheeks, sharp chin, burnt skin (or so said a communist), leaning over one of the works mentioned by the secret service, taking notes here and there, perhaps going up the stairs to the upper floor (because curious, as you yourself were, or to unearth who knows what writing), questioning a librarian or whispering to his deskmate. You weren't unaware, in roaming this library, that Nguyên had worked on his first book here: it's possible that you had already imagined him, if only for two or three seconds, as you do now for much longer.

A tranquil Place, decorous vehicles, this neat arrondissement, fifth of its kind.

"Project managers" (unless they're "account executives") are chuckling. And, over there, where your eyes come to rest, an orange Eiffel Tower lays into a more vivid sun, leaking, punctured, upon the rooftops below (the last time you'd seen it, this tower, was a recent Saturday: barricades were hastily raised along the Seine; one could hear sirens and scraping metal and the president's hated name; we went everywhere repeating that, of the rule of the wealthy, we'd had enough; everywhere strangers had for each other this smile, long forgotten, and it was this smile that law enforcement, moving forward behind shields, intended to rub from our faces).

The balconies of rue Soufflot are all alight, saffron-yellow stripes.

While the French Republic offered itself a new president for the next seven years (Paul Deschanel would resign that same year, depressed, on sedatives, picking flowers in the mud, having stepped out of a moving train while wearing pajamas), and Munich saw one corporal Hitler announce the twenty-odd points of his program (colonies, pure blood, an end to immigration, the nationalization of trust-owned companies), Nguyên wasn't staying idle. He composed a play in verse to reach his countrymen enlisted in the metropolitan army; translated Montesquieu in the Annamite language; finished his book; requested a preface from Marx's grandson—who, overwhelmed by the task, advised him first and foremost to stick one in the faces of the agents trailing him every day—and then from the editor of *L'Humanité*; charged a young artist with designing the cover, a map of Indochina harassed by a soldier; and received his quota of visitors at 6 villa des Gobelins, as well as mail from Cuba and England. He then, on May 1, condemned colonial expeditions in front of two thousand people in Kremlin-Bicêtre.

In Lyon, in Marseille, in Paris, the utmost was still being done to find out who hid behind this assumed name, the Patriot. A certainty, now, in the eyes of those charged with the State's security: the man had established himself as the center, the soul of the Annamite movement. Through the efforts of prefects or chiefs of this, directors or inspectors of that, the government eventually achieved its ends: it discovered his father's identity, an ousted mandarin and tippler from a family of peasants, and with it that of his son, Nguyên Tât Thanh, not an idiot, that's for sure, some knowledge of mechanics, and the sea calling to him one day in 1911.

Perhaps that particular summer was endowed with a distinctive yellow disc, a sun as if drawn, high above the rooftops. You don't know whether it was a summer like the one, delightful, that Tolstoy brought up one day in a letter to say that he was crazy about life, but at least you know that in it the standing ovations were never-ending. Lenin only began to speak once the hurrays and the bravos, dying down, allowed him to. You can imagine him without too much trouble, standing on the platform—by which you mean that his appearance is clear and detailed in your mind, his immense forehead and his squinting myopic eyes, the confidence that captures the attention in the rare footage of him shot during his lifetime, his one-point-sixty-five meters and his tie—striped, perhaps*—tucked under a thick waistcoat. If your daydream was cut short, there's at least this painting, three-by-five, signed Brodsky, which, though one more daub to blame on social realism, has the rare merit of showing what was at play that July 19. Not far from a pair of red flags, casting their shadows upon an oh-so-regal column, you recognize Gorky and, to the left of a clumsily included Lenin the orator, Trotsky, one row back, whispering in his neighbor's ear (Stalin must have forgotten to erase him).

And so it was on that summer day in Petrograd that Lenin spoke of the colonies. Pillaged, slaughtered by a handful of states and operators. He spoke of the Soviet revolution that would gain from spreading to the Orient, to Asia, to the four corners of the world. He spoke of the seventy percent of the human race, the tributaries, the captives, the faces on the ground, that Bolsheviks aspired to represent. He spoke of world proletarian revolution, he said these three words and you can imagine the pride overcoming him as he did so, in front of the delegates, more than two hundred of them, from everywhere, from Bulgaria, France, India, Korea, Mexico, attending the Second Congress of the Communist International. You would almost feel it, this pride, in reading reports from the meeting a century later: you need only

* Maybe this needs a footnote: Later, reading Marcel Cachin's *Carnets*, book II, you will learn that Lenin actually did wear a striped tie that July 19, 1920.

think of the world war, barely two years behind, of letters from infantrymen hoping that their feet would freeze so they could be evacuated, of the eyes of mangy horses wasted by the gases, of the hoofs of mules sinking in the mud, of messenger dogs caught in barbed wire, of widows left without even God to talk to, all of that the single, solitary fault of the powerful (you wrote "of the rich," first, and perhaps one shouldn't balk at such Christlike simplicity); you need only think of women bartering their bodies in the obscurity of moist bedrooms, of smoked-out indigènes, of black-skinned amputees, of girls in Tongking pinned under foreigners' genitalia, of kings, queens, magnates, usurers, speculators, shits in muslin and ascot ties, manure in gold-leafed makeup; you need only catch a glimpse of the gardens of great palaces and those there, in their millions, who were told things couldn't be any other way, property owners and beggars, that's how it is, such is life; there, for sure, is all you need to measure the exact weight of these three words, world proletarian revolution. You have reasons to hold Lenin at a distance from your heart, but you know why, at this very instant, the room could only erupt in raucous applause.

The Congress would stretch to three weeks, and, on August 7, Trotsky in turn took the floor. "We will hang on," he declared. In the name of the masses on their knees in Europe, in Asia, in all the meridians. In the name of the Arab and African communists he hoped would join them. Then he concluded, "Stick it in the back of world capital" — the blade of the revolution.

~

The SFIO had sent two activists. All the delegates stayed close to the Kremlin, at the Delovoy Dvor hotel—a wealthy industrialist had built it before getting murdered in 1918, under circumstances the inquisitive still need to untangle. Between its walls, three hundred rooms, electricity, hot water, a telephone, and the famous John Reed, who hadn't scribbled a book but a handbook, *Ten Days That Shook the World*, prefaced by Lenin himself. Reed suffered from scurvy and would soon die of typhus; his native America took this ballsucker of a bleeding heart for an undesirable, and Finnish law enforcement had just thrown him in a cell after rooting him out of a ship's coal bunker with a hundred diamonds or so in his pockets. More than just a novelistic veneer to that story; but there was also this Congress in four languages, official at that, Russian, German, French, and English, and the journalist had taken the opportunity to lend a hand in its organization.

When they weren't debating, the delegates went to the theater, went for walks in Moscow, or were invited to admire the benefits of volunteer work, which, as the president of the Council of People's Commissars asserted, allowed the replacement of "every man for himself" by "every man for all," free market by communist labor. No doubt there were some this rhetoric transfixed, while others were less inclined to join in. It's all very well to laugh, in the ease of time passed; if candor unfastens the world, cynicism nails it in place. They could also consult Trotsky's and Lenin's last two books, graciously left in their hotel room—from the latter, *"Left-Wing" Communism: An Infantile Disorder* (to summarize: iron Party, practical compromises, anarchist bastards).

And then there were Lenin's theses, him again, on the national and colonial questions. And so we return to Nguyên Ai Quôc.

"How I Chose Leninism," that's the title of an article Hô Chi Minh gave to a Soviet periodical in spring 1960, on the eve of his seventieth birthday.

"After the First World War, I eked out a living in Paris." His solidarity with the October Revolution wasn't solely a question of instincts, he would say. If he was fond of Lenin, this fondness grew unaware of his writings—the man had liberated the Russian people, that was enough for him.

At the time, what French socialists debated until one in the morning was whether or not they should join the communists; in other words, leave the Second International for the Third, established a year earlier in 1919. Hô Chi Minh would admit that he didn't know which of II or III to come down for, nor, eventually, which of the camps formed in the shadows of these Roman twiglets. The needle in his compass pointed only with great care, unflappably, in one direction: the fate of the colonies. A comrade gave him Lenin's theses to read, in the form of a draft, later published in two parts in the pages of *L'Humanité*, just a few days before the Congress opened in Petrograd.

And so he read them.

Admitted he didn't get everything.

But what he got, reading and rereading, was that communists cared about the colonies far more than socialists.

"What emotion, what enthusiasm," he would add. He cried. Alone in his room, he spoke aloud. Called out to an imaginary crowd that this was now the path to liberation.

It wouldn't be entirely devoid of sense to imagine Hô Chi Minh reconstructing this visitation after the fact—and this word, visitation, seems the right one to you: there is, in his tears, something of the collapsed zealot on his way to Damascus, of the dazed virgin called to sainthood. What could be more awe-inspiring, indeed, for legend and orthodoxy, than an apostle soaking the prophet's writings with his tears? But this hypothesis is worth no more than its reverse: it's entirely possible that this is what happened and that Hô Chi Minh, forty years later, was quite content to commit the memory to paper. A bare fact, that's all, as one recounts an anecdote by the warmth of a fireplace.

He therefore immediately sent his membership letter to the Third International.

A little too much grass pierces through the concrete at your feet. Large clouds are shuffling along, rubbing their shadows impudently on the street; a shaft of light hesitates to touch the hospital's outer walls. You cross paths with a nun, earthy veil and crinkled skin; she moves even more slowly than the folds of the flags out front; a rosary dangles, the sandals she wears have a Franciscan look about them. Farther on, on the flowery pediment of a disused entrance, you read "Practice respiratory tract Tuberculosis"; you walk the length of the building, rust-colored bricks, port windows, a dumpster in the courtyard; a man in green pants repairing a motorcycle, a small cardboard box filled with tools on the floor beside him. Farther still, vague passersby, an unassuming black dog; and even farther, finally, the Val-de-Grâce, its cross pitched into a low cloud.

It's here, in July 1920, Cochin hospital, bed 18, that Nguyên Ai Quôc arrived in order to cure a phlegmon in his right shoulder. A spy noted that a young woman of eighteen years, presented in a report as his mistress, regularly came to visit him.

Did she really share his daily life and his bed? Did he really give up a bit of that heart so entirely devoted to politics? Did he feel his life was entwined with another's, and that it would remain so even if time were to separate them, until the end of his own? Did he bear the weight of the absent body that only that body's return can relieve? Did he believe in shelter-like looks, round warmth, halting embrace, a haven from a world gone mad?

No one knows.

Or we know very little.

Three names come up: Marie Brière, Mademoiselle Bourdon—or Boudon—and Mademoiselle Rose. Here again, the conditional rules: Brière, seamstress, and Bourdon, communist, could be one and the same. According to a novelist who had her information from Lucie and Raymond Aubrac, friends of Hô Chi Minh, she was deported to Ravensbrück two decades after their separation. You contact the camp's survivors' association to try and find out more: to no avail: her name—but, if married, did she keep that name?—doesn't appear in the records of deaths at Ravensbrück, nor in the *Memorial-Book of Deportations from France*. Unless, that is, "Bourdon" was only a cover name, a ploy elaborated by Nguyên so as to mislead the intelligence services . . .

In a volume of his *Socialist History of the French Revolution*, Jaurès, bringing up Robespierre, cites a description of him authored by a deputy to the National Convention: "He liked neither women nor money"—only politics. In *Things Seen*, Hugo assigns a few lines to Blanqui, so severe that his prose isn't enough to redeem them. Of Blanqui the Confined, who himself had no fondness for Robespierre the Incorruptible, the writer said the following: "no infatuation, no love, no vice, no women." Adding: "One of these men who have only one idea."

Was Nguyên Ai Quôc made of this material—that with which our species sculpts its soldier-monks? Some would swear it of Hô Chi Minh, whose official portrait insists on depicting him as a speckless celibate, a patriarch without descent, driven solely by wisdom.

The president of the Vietnamese Republic, zealous ally of the North Americans, swore that Hô was "pure"—like Lucifer; Khrushchev ascribed an apostle's saintliness to him, in the most biblical sense; a French minister and an officer of the US Marine Corps said that he had absolute control over his emotions; a general deployed in the Indochina War asserted that his opponent was entirely selfless: all that mattered to him was the political task he set himself; Thorez's spouse wouldn't have denied it, admitting after his death that the Vietnamese man gave the impression of living solely for independence and socialism; and the director of programming for French television in the 1950s confirms it: a water-drinker who believed in the revolution.

Psychologizing history is blasphemy, we know; there's nonetheless little doubt that September 11, 1973, wouldn't have been the same had Allende been Castro. Underlying structures no more erase flesh than social relations do inner man. To grasp at once the modes of production and the missed opportunities seems to you a slop to dip your pen in. His brothers and his enemies sketched a similar portrait: Hô Chi Minh was a calm man, serious, spartan, punctual, obstinate, diplomatic, firm, concrete, courteous, focused, and endowed with a singular power of persuasion. Some, if fewer of them, also reported his excessive pride, his duplicity, his acting talent—delineating more than the intrinsically sage or Confucian saint that his aura pointed to—his harshness and authoritarianism; all, and such a consensus is never reached without embarrassment, insisted on shedding light on his simplicity, his tact, his gentleness, his charm, his sensibility, his kindness, his bonhomie, his mischievousness, his naïveté, his humor, his thoughtfulness, his loyalty, his disinclination toward violence, and his clear hostility toward protocol. A word recurs over and over again in the mouths of figures otherwise little given to his cause: humanist. A French minister—another—went so far as to call him endearing; a Russian interpreter remembered a passionate person, thorough and sorrowful; the poet Osip Mandelstam himself noticed a delicate and tactful man.

Enough.

One day, at the foot of the Kremlin Wall, you saw Lenin's embalmed body, daubed for all eternity in quinine and acetic acid (somewhere in *My Life*, Trotsky wrote that such a presentation offended one's conscience and made it possible to betray Lenin's ideas in order to honor his memory). Hô Chi Minh's corpse suffered, against his will—the ashes of his burnt body should've been scattered, with no ruinous funeral, on a pretty hill—a similar pitiful fate: granite mausoleum, marble columns, precious woods, soft lighting, military guard of honor. Listing the deceased's virtues tends henceforth toward the farcical. What's more, you overstepped the bounds you had set for yourself: Hô Chi Minh isn't your concern, but Nguyên Ai Quôc.

The minister for the colonies tasked the Paris Police prefecture with tightening surveillance on the young Asian man, who for a while stopped retouching photographs to dedicate himself to the decoration of Chinese frescoes in the middle of the Latin Quarter. Bus trips and conferences, visits to the laundry and the post office, purchases at local businesses: the "revolutionary agitator," as he was now referred to in reports, became the subject of incessant attention. The individuals he welcomed to his home were listed, the contents of the newspapers he received inventoried.

During this time, four thousand five hundred kilometers to the east, meridian forty-nine and something, the world communist revolution attempted to give itself a structure in Azerbaijan: in Baku opened, that September 1920, a Congress for which the label "historic" isn't excessive. More than two thousand delegates, seven sessions, one single goal: extend the struggle to the Orient. In Germany, the red flag had just been thrown down the deepest depths of a canal; in Hungary, the same. And Soviet Russia, thus surrounded, couldn't remain isolated: it was the whole world, united, that had to be liberated from the power of money. Fight the oppressors: such was the opening order in Baku—the proletariat from industrialized countries fighting alongside colonized peoples and victims of imperialism.

One of Hô Chi Minh's biographers would write that Nguyên Ai Quôc was part of it—nothing, however, would lead one to believe so. A few days after the Congress ended, the French police summoned him in. He tried to mislead them, referring to deceased parents and presenting himself as a farmer, assuring them that his pen and birth names were the same, swearing that the date of his birth was indeed the one he'd had written on his identity card a year prior—you have little doubt the police didn't believe a word. Nguyên professed that he felt French and had arrived in the metropole in June or July 1919: that date, as already mentioned, is one on which the intelligence services relied—that would make it, strangely, the only correct information garnered from his interrogation.

A dispatch from the minister of the colonies, come straight from Indochina, ordered the French authorities to hinder Nguyên's plans should the idea of going home cross his mind. The future "Franciscan Gandhi," a phrase we owe another biographer, well and truly scared them. Within the next few weeks, he would speak out in the press against the sending of Annamite contingents to Syria and denounce the metropole's dirty deeds—famine and cannon fire. He would also press Marcel Cachin to assist him in publishing his book: in vain. The editor-in-chief of *L'Humanité* wouldn't write his preface, nor would he mobilize his newspaper to publish it; the reason: Europeans aren't all that interested in Indochina.

The sky is like a sea the wind forgot. Not a crease, a polished stone. In the square, trickles of water dribble out of a fountain by the dozen; the neighborhood youth lunch on a corner of thick grass; a few pigeons walk among the shadows unfurled by chestnut trees; burrs and their seeds are scattered about the patchy grass; a man without money sleeps, lying on a bench. The pavement glistens, freshly washed by a city employee. One would almost forget that this street, Richelieu, saw barricades raised in 1830, housed Fourier, hid the engineer Vuillaume when Versailles was shooting on sight, and crossed paths with Lenin riding a bicycle, pinched soon after.

A mottled tent shields the body it shelters from the eyes of passersby—banana boxes are used as a doormat. Another body is crossing the street nearby, a blue-collared shirt sticking out of a sweater the same color, and a bottle of sparkling water in hand. Women in heels knock along the pavement, a Siberian husky ambles by.

You enter, after the customary security check, the Bibliothèque nationale. Courtyard, hall, reading room. Visitors, separated by a long aisle, turn pages, take notes, tap keys on their keyboards. Light falls equally on all points from nine ceramic cupolas. You stop for a moment to look at the cast-iron columns, the men of letters in profile on medallions, the somewhat silly paintings. Walls covered with books, domed table lamps. Under your feet the oak flooring creaks—redone, since Nguyên last tread on it. It was beneath these cupolas that he worked on his manuscript almost daily, *Indochina* (no longer *The Oppressed*).

But this text, whatever the title, was never published.

Or else reworked in such a way that we don't know if it's the same project: *The Case Against French Colonization*, on the shelves of French bookstores by the mid-1920s. Nguyên was already gone by then, wandering Red Square alongside the president of the Comintern, or chatting with Mandelstam. That century and its demented features: the next decade, Stalin would make these two disappear.

The book you bought a long time ago at a yearly fête organized by the newspaper Jaurès founded. Worn spine, since then, here and there loose pages held together with tape, pencil marks everywhere. Not so far from a prayerbook. A decree had just struck a paragraph down in a law that, in 2005, still praised the positive influence of the French overseas presence—a minister by the name of Sarkozy, destined for the office of president of the Republic, and for charges of corruption and influence-peddling, had naturally spoken out against supporters of "repentance": doubtless he hadn't taken the time to open this book.

A few streets from the library, a bar.

You order a coffee at the counter and take another book out of your bag. "I had left Paris, then a mass ossuary, I thought the great city dead: but today I see that Paris is awake," you read: a speech by Louise Michel, returned from deportation to Kanaky. One hundred and thirty-nine years later, this sentence lives again, come what may: insurrectionary fire on the Champs-Élysées, calls under your very eyes for bread, and even to arms, defying the soldiery and the imperial arch, the image of the capital you had in your mind, black and bereaved in winter 2015, is rearranged. Erecting barricades will never wash away the blood spilled by theocrats; doing so nonetheless raises the bodies extinguished, put down, banished by the rule of gold.

A year after the attacks, a journalist wrote, in a voluminous work dedicated to Paris, that the terrorists were the children of revolutionaries, among whom he named, in an extensive passage, Nguyên Ai Quôc. Scum sometimes aspires to the label of profession.

You know the lesson, masses are the makers of history, and so it is in every language. But while you must admit that you find the pictures of a lifeless Guevara stomach-churning, you forget the names of his comrades stretched out below the washing sink in Vallegrande where his executioners laid him: disheveled, head back, hands shackled over his pelvis, felled before his fortieth year, hair a mess, formalin in his aorta, superb of dirty beard. Though you grant sociologists that the story of a single existence, even one that includes the significant events and connections necessary to any biographical undertaking, is as pointless as the story of a train journey written without knowledge of the entire rail network, still, knowing that George Orwell simply enjoyed watching the eggs of forked-tail caterpillars delights you. To talk of the self while society believes in it alone deserves at least a word of apology; when the singular rules, literature must head the opposition — in lowering the heads that stick out. Your only defense, for now: for Nguyên Ai Quôc, the first person is plural.

At the end of the 1940s, the book *Glimpses of the Life of Hô Chi Minh* was published in China. Strange, saintly fate: is this, as the foreword claims, the biographical work of a historian by the name of Trân Dân Tiên, or that, autobiographical, of Hô Chi Minh himself, whose legendary modesty might as a result be severely defaced? You won't answer the question, which still divides French and Vietnamese historians. But you read the accounts that one (his sole publication) and the other (whose Party press tallied in 2015 the hundred and seventy-five names Nguyen used during his lifetime) made of socialist meetings in which they or Nguyên took part. Against the endless talk of his comrades, he offered substance: aren't socialists and communists all revolutionaries? Isn't unity more important than controversy? Such naïveté made his audience smile. Typical of the novice, sure, but maybe more: the young man was down-to-earth, practical and empirical, of a type that moves forward with hands outstretched. He would remain like this. There's no text or witness that doesn't confirm it: theory made him sweat, angels dancing on a pin, yawn—one can still find Leninists, Trotskyists, or Guevarists, but no suffix is attached to the Vietnamese president's name, and that's no coincidence.

That's also how he rubbed shoulders with groups usually pulling faces at one another, if not sometimes making war. Chatting with the anarchos, Marxist gatekeepers, and clean-nailed social democrats, publishing in the pages of the *Libertaire* and the *Bulletin communiste*, hopping from the doctrinal points of some to others' blasphemies, zigzagging between the tracks, neglecting totems and guardrails. Bastard in his amateurism, hybrid by temperament, mixed-blood for lack of time: Nguyên knocked about between cats and dogs. And that, you have to admit, you find extremely endearing. All the more because you're not unaware that the revolutionary would, more than twenty years later and by then custodian of the Party's words, declare that comrades who don't toe the line must be broken. And you would like to have never read it, this sentence uttered in a private conversation, you would like to forget it, this ugly verb, to break. Or be able to act as if you had. Worse: you're perfectly well aware of the existence of an eight-point report, the fourth point of which insists on the "political extermination" of Trotskyists. And nothing casts a shadow over you quite like fratricidal blood. Nothing, among the centuries you drag about with you, saddens you more than Desmoulins's sentence, signed by the very man who had been a witness to his wedding; than the Commune tearing itself apart between committees and minorities while Versailles blockaded the capital; than Barcelona tallying in May the bodies of insurgents as Fascism shouted on its doorstep; than Jeanson directing a "beautiful soul" at Camus while the latter directed a "Monsieur le directeur" at his friend Sartre. "A rebel is a rebel," or so said, rightly, the poet Aragon—to better forget his history with Nizan. You know, of course, that stark contrasts don't make for united fronts, that an enemy was never enough to close ranks, that to smile at slogans is still very much the hipster's art. You believe no less that it's only right to listen to an ally until dawn when the ogre shows his teeth; that disunity is a luxury to which the Earth doesn't yet have the right; that one must find in the day what night tells us and in night what the day reveals. The Trotskyist Ta Thu Thâu succumbed to the blows of the Party the day after independence: Hô Chi Minh swore he cried for him but gave himself a reason, that of the State, about which the errant he was in Paris still didn't know a thing.

And so came the time for a clean break.

This took place in Tours, toward the end of the year 1920, steps from a church converted, in the wake of the French Revolution, into a stable.

If humanity is the scene on which the struggle between partisans and opponents of equality is played out, and has been ever since life, having left the warm seas, took for itself opposable thumbs, upright posture, and conceptual language—and we have every right to believe that the very existence of our species, one step removed from the animal within, has for itself no justification other than to one day prevail in this old duel—then it was on the shores of the rivers Loire and Cher that a new act strove to be written.

On the lips of a sharing France, come to attend this congress below a banner on which large white letters trumpeted "Workers of the World, Unite," just one question: how to advance the struggle against those who, capitalists or nationalists from France and the wider world, thought that one human being could be worth less than another?

More than three hundred delegates had made the trip. More than four thousand mandates, and everywhere the shadow cast by the late Jaurès.

Within this audience of black hats, there was Léon Blum, the offspring of Abraham and Adèle. You can make out his long gentlemanly silhouette, bright eyes underneath a thin pince-nez, voice high-pitched, cracked and trembling. Charles Maurras had yet to call him a piece of trash fit only for getting shot in the back, no more than he'd instituted paid annual leave, under popular pressure, or been handed over to the Germans by a Maréchal, to be placed in house arrest on Buchenwald's doorstep. You think you can see deputy Marcel Cachin, solid Breton head and the appropriate whiskers, who, returned from Russia four months prior, had in his notebooks written of the need to act alongside Moscow, so much was the future, and life in general, at play there, on the Money Regime's ashes. You look for Nguyên Ai Quôc, of course, the only imperial subject present during these few days, and there he is, large forehead, flattened black hair, cheeks like two pebbles from a sandless beach, and an elegant double-breasted suit—far from the "vagrant monk" alluded to, years later, by General Leclerc's former press officer when he met our conference-goer turned president. And then, amid this male audience said to be working for the human race despite the absence of its other half, you recognize Clara Zetkin, whom you would like not to have to sketch but it so happens that she's omitted once a year, every March 8, you mean, though she was just as much of an instigator.

The Congress was spread over five days and included, forsooth, official reports, keen applause, appeals, uproars, exclamations, varied movements, interruptions, laughter, irony, accusations of obfuscation, Marx citations, and full-throated chanting. Vaillant-Couturier said the debate is grueling; Cachin said Russia is an immense and prodigious event; Blum expressed his clear and wholehearted support for the dictatorship of the proletariat, but also his opposition, clear as well, wholehearted as well, to Bolshevik military command and to the little interest the Bolsheviks have in freedom of thought; Frossard said socialism is arming the people. As for Nguyên Ai Quôc, he said, in his capacity as "delegate for Indo-China," that his country is the prey of capital, opium, and alcohol; that its prisons are filled to the brim; and that freedom is there but an empty word. He called for the Socialist Party to act in favor of the colonized and, immediately upon being interrupted, he hurled back, mischievously, a demand for the dictatorship of silence. The thirty-year-old informed them of his wish to join the Third International, and upon a second interruption, snapped back a disarming "Silence, parliamentarians!"—how distant, suddenly, seems the Montmartre mute ... Finally, in the name of all of humanity, a poignant plea: "Comrades, save us!"

Twelve minutes, without notes.

The Tours Congress applauded; the press would allude to him without naming him; his intervention would remain unnoticed, commented one of his biographers.

And then they shouted Long live Jaurès and Lenin, they sang the revolution and votes were counted: just over three thousand in favor of falling in step behind Moscow, about one thousand for the preservation of the old socialist home.

The police had tried to stop Nguyên from giving a speech—in vain, then.

~

Two months later, signs of him again, holed up in the bed of a room at the Cochin hospital, Pasteur Wing. Poorly fed, poorly treated, he wrote. Asked for cheese, butter, and soap from a close relation. Recommended the reading of anarchist newspapers.

A secret agent of Vietnamese origin introduced himself to Nguyên as a former wartime interpreter. "If I'm interested in politics, it's because I fear neither death nor prison," the patient told him in return. Nguyên added that his friends, distinguished socialist officials, would know how to defend him if there was trouble—we know he was aware that he was constantly spied upon; we're not sure whether he manipulated all the strangers that came to see him: this exchange nonetheless clearly looks like a warning. He explained that in Indochina he would've been beheaded, but that on the mainland he was able to defend the entirety of his claims. The revolutionary finally admitted that he dreamed of establishing a real organization: strength in numbers, so that others, should he fall, could replace him.

A nurse put an end to the visit.

That spring, an article he penned appeared in *La revue communiste*.

Despite their vocal commitment and the split that took place in Tours—a proof of purpose, supposedly—Nguyên criticized the communists' inaction vis-à-vis the colonies. Indochina wasn't ready for revolution, he admitted, but it would be wrong to claim that it was satisfied with imperial rule. Furthermore, he complained of the prohibition on reading Rousseau, Montesquieu, or Hugo, and rose up once again against the stupefaction of the population with drink and opiates, against repression by guillotine, exile, or the cell. His people, subdued "on the altar of the Good Lord Capitalism," wouldn't fail to follow Russia, China, and India: under their apparent submissiveness, rumblings. Capitalism had prepared the soil for revolt; it was left to socialism to "sow the seed of emancipation."

You look up the corresponding intelligence report: this article is "extremely concerning" and could have significant fallout—it therefore deserves "the utmost attention."

The Empire created race to teach the faithful why doing far away what no one in their heart could endorse at home is a good thing. Hitler made the concept his, then cheated distances: what liberal Europe offered to savages, the Reich did to subhumans. We're beating around the bush so as not to jump in: Hitler is Evil, but he was our glory so long as he struck outside our clime. The German was a zealous student: he carried out under our eyes the work we reserved for imperial frontiers. His gaze is chilling because we know, without completely admitting it to ourselves, that he's our mirror image: the German never kept his bright idea a secret: to play cowboys and Indians and turn a whole chunk of Europe into, as he spelled out clearly, "what India was for England."

In Paris, that May 29, 1921, communists, socialists, and anarchists gathered by the thousands at the Père Lachaise cemetery in memory of fallen Communards—the same day, in Bombay, Gandhi called for funds to be raised to help organize the struggle for independence. Flags, briar roses in buttonholes, flower crowns. Maimed veterans parading. Dockers, railroad workers. They shouted Down with war, they shouted Long live Louise Michel. Then they crossed paths with a clerical procession and from both sides swear words were hurled like so many rocks. The police charged in, aimed blows, made the horses' hooves clatter. Nguyên was roughed up but managed to escape; others were clubbed, even in cafés: a fondness, no doubt, for the job well done.

How could the colonized (colonials, at the time) organize on the mainland? Fruit of the fusion of two collectives, Indochinese and Malagasy, the Intercolonial Union was born two months later in answer to that very question. Nguyên Ai Quôc was clearly counted among its founders. According to the police, the idea of an alliance first took root in a worker cooperative in the 13th arrondissement, 28 boulevard Arago. You go there. The chalky sky hangs from chestnut trees, a great silence at their feet; you pass by a plump woman in a pink top, so pink that you come to doubt having seen it; she's walking a little dog, ranting, why do they like breaking bottles, really I don't understand, she's ranting right next to you in the hope, no doubt, that you might wholeheartedly agree with, or simply hear, her. The animal had indeed almost put a paw down on a shard of glass. Instead of the old scheming company, you come face to face with a stationery shop.

The Union soon had something like two hundred members from all over the cosmopolitan Paris of the interwar era. It didn't have a strict policy line: reformers and revolutionaries, nationalists and communists, assimilationists and supporters of independence rubbed shoulders more or less comfortably. The French Communist Party, pressured by the Comintern to bring the colonized into the Marxist fold, wouldn't be long in funding it.

"Is the Communist regime suitable for Asia in general and Indochina in particular?" Nguyên had in fact asked in a monthly run by a former member of the SFIO, only to answer immediately in the affirmative, even adding that the liberation of Asians, unjustly taken for inferiors, would help their Western brothers at their own task—but fate put on a mocking smile: at the same time, Stalin, twelve years older than the Vietnamese, asserted for his part in the pages of *Pravda* that "advanced" nations liberated, in liberating themselves, "backward" people.

Such political maturity was far from universal within the Dragons. To such an extent that disagreements eventually got the better of the group, at villa des Gobelins, in mid-July. This was what one might call a hell of a row: Nguyên apparently left the premises escorted by police officers, to live for a few days with another countryman in the 13th arrondissement, 12 rue Buot (today: three-story housing, outdoor wall lights, paved alley, graffiti on the walls).

Afterward, with the help of socialist friends, he whom Kateb Yacine would name "the man in the rubber sandals," "the man of shore and shadows," "the sweeper and the strategist," "the pariah whose head was held so high," moved alone into a miserable abode on the other side of the city, due north.

"The Annamite agitator NGUYEN AI QUOC has moved out of N°6 villa des Gobelins permanently to live in a hotel 9 impasse Compoint, where he inhabits a small room with a monthly rent of 40 Frs payable in advance."

A report dated July 29.

A suspicious package, at Place de Clichy station, forces you to retrace your steps, or at least leave the premises without delay. Law enforcement on patrol at the metro entrance. On the avenue's sidewalk, a bushy old man, stooping, clothed in a colored tunic, taps on a mobile phone. Seated in an office chair; his bundle—a mass of plastic bags—is tied to the stroller he keeps next to himself.

You make a stop at L'Étoile de Clichy. Customers talk to each other in Berber; a radio mumbles through a commercial break; the bartender—face like it was carved with a knife, blue almond eyes—takes a few drags from an e-cigarette. Pictures of African-American militants compete for space at the back of the room.

It's there, just there, at the angle formed by the bistro, that a barricade, the last in the neighborhood to fall, was raised during the Commune. To defend it: a dry cleaner, a professor of Sanskrit, the editor of the paper *L'Ami du Peuple*, and good old Gustave Lefrançais, dedicatee of "The Internationale," a republican for whom the Republic was only worth it so long as it worked toward the abolition "of all privileges."

You continue walking beneath a sky so white it doesn't deserve the name. A man sleeps under a bus stop, wrapped in blankets; a dislocated toilet sits in passage Legendre. You make a left, and then another left. Villa Compoint—a dead end until 1994—stretches for less than a hundred meters: Nguyên lived here for two years.

The road is paved, deserted, dotted with flowering pear trees. At number 4, a bookshop, Résistances, was vandalized a decade ago by a pro-Israeli militia. At 9, the edifice in which Nguyên lived is no more: demolished in 1998 and replaced by a shapeless apartment block, boasting twelve units.

A teenager stops you, asking for the reasons behind your interest in this building, saying he lives in the building next door. You summarize the matter in three words: he points to a plaque, in a recess to the right of a door surrounded by two mopeds, that he's certain you'll be interested in: Here from 1921 to 1923 lived and campaigned for the independence and freedom of the Vietnamese people and other oppressed peoples Nguyên Ai Quôc, known under the name Hồ Chí Minh—underneath, in smaller font, the date it was put up: January 1983. A sign, the first. The man was said to be elusive, fleeting, ubiquitous; some said they even doubted his very existence. So you haven't totally lost your mind: your ghost was.

The teenager adds that he likes the flowers that adorn the plaque—red geraniums—and is happy to take, as the photographer he'd like to become someday, pictures of them with that phone that never leaves his hand. An adult passes, a family member, whom the teenager—you can't quite tell if he's a boy or a girl, but who cares—addresses and informs of your situation, a historian, or something like that, searching for an Indian emperor who lived here. Or something like that.

A campaign poster, torn, hangs across the bookshop, whose door you open to ask the woman at the counter if she knows that Hô Chi Minh lived only a few meters away. She sure does, but you thought she might, though she didn't find out, she specifies, until a very belated trip to Vietnam.

A book published in Hanoi, that you in fact acquired there, shows his business card: "Photographic Portrait-Enlargements." The address that detains you today appears on it, along with his name, spelled thus: "Nguyên Aï Quâc." There's also a picture of number 9 as he would've known it: a hovel on two levels, like those depicted in verses from Queneau ("Leprous homes / choleric homes / afflicted homes / Shit-stained abodes"). The young man lived on the first floor; a room, a bed, a table, a dresser, an oil lamp, a wash bowl; no electricity, a window with swing shutters— he had to stretch his neck just to see a bit of sun or moon. The neighbors hung their laundry upon taut clotheslines, he washed his outside, and to his visitors offered jasmine tea and green vegetables cooked with soy. Not too hard to imagine him here.

It's this same address that you find in an ad that appeared at the time in *La Vie ouvrière*: "If you want vivid memories of friends or family, get your photos enlarged at NGUYEN A.-Q., 9, impasse Compoint (17th). Good portrait, good frame, from 45 fr."

And it's in this very street, fifteen years later, the Spanish Civil War won by fascists, that Victor Serge, escaped from Stalinist Russia and soon to be in Mexican exile, showed up at POUM headquarters to work to free its incarcerated militants. You went to look for his grave in Mexico, by the way: nameless, dusty, move along. Hi there, old boy! heart out of whack, holed shoes in an old jalopy, the century in pieces before your very eyes. A map is a frieze, time condensed into space. Geography of events, topography of facts: no doubt you go about lugging, like a simple mule, what Hugo called—before Péguy ever did—this "dark loyalty to fallen things."

The dead end fades behind your back.

A busted clothesline leans on a facade, a woman smokes on a balcony, a man is double-parked in order to buy pastries. Leaves crumple under your heels, and pigeons, with their wings, are practicing the various forms of the verb "to flap." The metro car is packed; a young man launches into a rap song for a few coins.

In Montreuil, you'll have a look at a few relics from his abode in impasse Compoint—museumified after it was demolished. The white sink in which he washed his battered hands, the cracked blue plaque bearing number 9, the wooden door that saw him come and go. "Sacred" objects, according to a framed statement by a former Party general secretary.

Nonbelievers appear to be holding on to two or three fantasies.

~

Boris Souvarine appeared in the pages of the magazine *Est & Ouest* in the mid-1970s to say that he had met Nguyên in Paris in 1917. According to him, the emigrant lived some-where near Montmartre—rue Marcadet, perhaps, unless it was in this "somber hotel" in a cul-de-sac that you couldn't find. Souvarine, who had opposed the Sacred Union and fought in the Marne, revealed that he had himself signed Nguyên up for the SFIO, and guided him as he took his first steps. He remembered a shy boy, gentle, unassuming, silent and fascinated by orators: "insignificant," in short (a nondescript man, without a past, whose conversation was "not in the least interesting," he added with contemptu-ous insistence). He also spoke of the transformation he had noticed, in person, at the Club du Faubourg: on this socialist stage, Nguyên had tamed his nerves, gained in poise, quickly become "someone."

Like Nguyên, Souvarine had rallied to communism in Tours—before being excluded from the Comintern and then the Party, of which he was a well-known figure, in part because he had published a pamphlet written by Trotsky. "In truth, Hô Chi Minh in no way resembled Nguyen Ai Quac," concluded this most stubborn loather of Stalinist barbarism. A break, not a continuum. A disavowal, not an evolution. Thus he never forgave his Vietnamese friend for not splitting with Moscow.

And so, yes.

One would need to return to the land as soon as the task was done: return the power taken so as to never be taken by it. Martyrs have the bitter privilege of not disappoint-ing: perhaps it's because Rosa Luxemburg never had the pleasure of being a minister that you noticed her name, not long ago, on the wall of a village in the mountains of Zapatista Chiapas. The magnetism of ruins? The romanticism of trinkets? Nay. Be that as it may: our victories weigh as heavily on our shoulders as our defeats; the defeated enlighten us, but the victors test us. If the rebel intoxicates, the revolutionary impedes: few can resist the first—poet at the break of day, pugilist when the sun falls beneath the rocks, escaping in cargo ships or on the roadside, a rusty shooter at his hip, careening heart as large as can be. We like the maverick, the eternal insurgent, fringes and freedom; we like Rimbaud and it costs us little: he's dead. But we look upon the revolutionary as one might hold a cigarette for the friend who stepped away: not entirely sure what to do with it. It's that there's both military and missionary under his skin, ideas undeviating and a world that goes round only if the greats are included together, comrades and enemies alike. If the first is accountable only to himself, the other embraces humanity as a whole. Both reside within you willy-nilly. And the fact is: the rebel is wary of revolutions, which always perish because of a lack of rebellion. The Vietnamese Communist regime shot innocents, locked up others for their opinions, crushed any and all criticism, falsified numbers, forced into exile some of its most loyal servants, and, like the hated capitalists, concentrated power at the top: to take down two empires and pick a people up from the rubble, we please ask that democrats shut up—and that the lock stay locked once peace is attained.

If, the Indochina War come to an end and Vietnam's forging ahead, Hô Chi Minh continued to delay the agrarian reforms expected in Moscow and Beijing, on the grounds that force is harmful and hot soup must be drunk in small sips, if the first Vice President of the Chinese Communist Party took him for a "rightist" and Stalin thought him a "troglodyte," if Raymond Aubrac wrote that no one ever saw him give an order to anyone, if it turns out that he chose to live in a caretaker's home rather than a palace, if he found himself progressively shut out from a power he had wanted to be collegial, until he became, to quote an American biographer, "a fly trapped in amber," in the minority of his own party, almost powerless, as if spitting in the wind, the mummified symbol of national reunification, a paternalistic old uncle reduced to touring schools, farms, and factories so as to spread the Word, if he admitted to linking up with the USSR because it was quite simply the only world power to offer him help against the savagery of colonial and capitalist civilization, if he was, according to some, guilty of cowardice in letting those more zealous than he hold the reins of state, if he replied to the all-powerful Mao that killing isn't moral when the latter replied that that's not the issue, if he publicly apologized in the summer of 1956 for the crimes committed by his regime as part of reforms that, as General Giap said, "executed too many honest people," if he confessed to having then lacked democratic spirit, and if he gave a definition of communism all should find uncomfortable to forsake—"No one will again be exploited, we will love one another and all be equal"—his name seems forever associated, like a monolith planted upright, with the disaster of a brief political experience that you lament more intimately than any choirboy for free enterprise: this failure still hinders the idea, nonetheless paramount, of a fundamental revision of the time-honored order everywhere ruling over us—that of the strong.

And so, yes, you could decide to cut the man in half, rebel and revolutionary, and keep only the half about which lively tales are told, the better to cast aside the troublemaker whose thought was carved into article 4 of the constitution of the current Socialist Republic of Vietnam. You could, if you didn't recognize a certain writerly cowardice in that. Against the violence of states, always first, the rebel's admirable integrity hits a wall: crown, knout, and sjambok only stand down at the sight of the word *revolution*.

All you've got to do now is make way with the wanderer and the political machinist he isn't quite yet, assume the tension without seeking synthesis, and recall, one more time, that no one writes without the knot vibrating somewhere in them.

Winter 1921.

Nguyên was laid off from the photo retouching studio that employed him at number 7 of the dead end on which he lived, because of his tuberculosis. And when he wasn't looking into the situation in India (much later, Hô Chi Minh would claim to be a student of Gandhi, in his own way, and pay a lengthy visit to Gandhi's tomb before planting there a frangipani from his homeland), he went almost every night to party branch meetings. Passing through Marseille, he called for the creation of an anticapitalist movement in Indochina and wanted, with his comrades, to endow the Intercolonial Union with a monthly voice: a magazine.

Stalin had just been elected general secretary of the Central Committee of the Communist Party, and Marseille, again Marseille, had opened its Colonial Exhibition, the nation's fifth, in the presence of the former governor-general of French Indochina: eighty-six acres and rickshaws to roam around in. The first issue of *Le Paria*, as it was called, came out April 22, 1922. A print run of a thousand copies—most of which were destined for the colonized territories. That same day, *Le Petit Parisien*'s headline read, "The struggle continues unabated," in Dublin as in Belfast: republicans were attempting to take a military barracks and occupy a wireless telegraph office. You also learn that in Rome, fascists paraded in the streets.

Nguyên didn't just write in the pages of *Le Paria* (and more so than anyone else): he illustrated it with his drawings, choice caricatures, done head-on, formally clumsy. He would admit one day: "I did almost everything." Including looking for readers.

Paris drapes itself in a blue that can only announce the night.

You cross Saint-Germain-des-Prés, once again immediately forgotten. Rue Jacques-Callot. On the corner, the sounds of a café-restaurant—it is said that Cézanne once parked his behind on one of its chairs, which is what you find charming about it, this uncouth Aixois and his brilliant fingers. Lights smudge in yellow the facade of an art gallery.

Two cyclists pass by, car paint glistens. The offices of the magazine *Clarté*, co-founded in the wake of the Great War by Barbusse and Vaillant-Couturier, were located here: they hosted *Le Paria*'s team in its early days. A black double door, two ringed knockers, a door code; a small business specializing in illustrated books, answering to the same address, adjoins the building entrance. Iron curtain lowered, lights on the second floor.

Moving on.

You didn't know this poem, surprisingly.

From Pasolini, you mean. The Italian had a column, "Chaos," in the weekly *Tempo*; he had planned on publishing the poem in issue thirty-eight, September 20, 1969. Why that never happened, you know not: the French translator is content with describing it as unpublished. Hô Chi Minh had died eighteen days earlier at the age of seventy-nine (the regime, lying, would announce it one day late); the writer wanted to set forth a few verses in his memory. No doubt it would be suitable to cite the poem whole, but full citations have a tendency to be, let's say, a pain in the ass. "You are the last public figure / that the world has loved; the last for which we cry. / [. . .] Your inhuman firmness upon which / the smile of so sweet / an old father was a mask / [. . .] You will not see the red flag become a flag / like any other."

Your attachment to Pasolini, pen and grit all in one, makes precious this likely essential poem: the confirmation, if need be, that even a literary life can hardly ignore the former train conductor, arrayed in a hundred and seventy-five names, who traversed the last century to cut it in half.

Le Paria's editorial team moved a thirty minutes' walk to the south, to 3 rue du Marché-des-Patriarches, in the 5th arrondissement. It's to this address, and to the name Nguyên Ai Quôc, that subscription forms were now supposed to be sent. A person called Bui Lam, sailor's son and former cabin boy on a cargo ship, would recount, in *Memories of Hô Chi Minh*, that reading *Le Paria* left him troubled and teary-eyed. This magazine made him want to act but he wasn't sure how; the idea came to him to knock at this address.

Single-story housing by a flea market. An excerpt from the periodical on the postbox. Two rooms, the bare essentials: one long table covered in newspapers in many languages, a few chairs, a planisphere on the wall. Upon entering the premises, he saw two North Africans at work; where Vietnam should be on the map, fingerprints, signs of wear, pencil marks. You imagine Nguyên tirelessly pointing out to his visitors the distance separating them from the place his heart beats for.

Ulysses—the other one, not the poet's—was at the time on display in bookshop stalls; you approach the window of one of them and find a reprint of Ritsos's *Monstrous Masterpiece*. (Come on, "Comrades of the World"!) An elephant is painted on a low wall to protest against worldwide poaching, a woman begs with what little part of her body isn't covered in rags, a sign for rue Marché-des-Patriarches is blanketed in stickers—again, you read the word "anarchist." Two workers in uniform are talking, the smoke from their cigs tangled up in frank, mustachioed noses; one of them is resting on a broom which, their walk resumed, will be dragged, *fr fr*, on the asphalt; a young man, blond, blue-jeaned and sneakered, is decorating the facade of his restaurant while chewing gum. You stop at number 3: below your feet, cigarette butts and crumpled metro tickets; on the ground floor, a psychiatrist's practice. And so it's here that Nguyên Ai Quôc read Michelet and Proudhon to his exiled brothers and that a magazine was put together despite the authorities' obstruction, more or less monthly to tell the truth: a large page all of words threaded together and sometimes drawings, words that the Vietnamese writer felt best to nestle inside humble hearts, not words with which one might embellish brilliant pink lips, not words with which to reduce to silence those who lack them, not words to make fictions to softly pass the time, no, words to fire one shot, only one, at the column, and see a back make like a reed when the wind finally shuts up, straighten, that's right, straighten up, with eyes to follow the act and at last crash into others', into the eyes of those swollen with diplomas and medals, twenty-five cents for these words and a title in French in Chinese in Arabic, going from ship's hold to sunlight, flying covertly to the four corners of the hemisphere, Madagascar Dahomey Maghreb Oceania Indochina, and it is said, and you believe it, that in the metropole Annamite workers bought it not knowing anything of the language, of pronouns, auxiliary verbs, of the hard g of "guêpe" and not of "givre," of the words "arpent" and "portefaix," "roulure" and "alambic," "frimas" and "ruffian," they bought it simply because they knew that *Le Paria* had a strong smell, that's right, an aura, resistant, impudent, taking to the streets, and they had their French pals, Lucien Émile or Jacquot, read it to them, this paper, the same that a young man took to Kanaky or Réunion after Nguyên told him to show solidarity with the French people, the working class, and all of the Earth's colonized—and when he came back, this young man, the revolutionary, who moved into this very building before he left France, would ask him to do more. But come on, now: these days there's only the blue of a glass window, here, the silence and what you might like to sneak into it.

To be a pilgrim is to be in league with big ideas: devotion, saintliness, grace, essence, the quest for meaning. Remnants and debris are for them so many entry points into the transcendent, the vast mysteries. But your gait is made of cruder steps: those of a miseducated mammal, an unrefined materialist (the body fails, and that's that). Sure, a stone can fossilize and yet retain evidence of some spirit, of some ancient breath, an indelible halo: a limpet. For you, pilgrimages, even secular, aren't the point; you create a herbarium, at the most: find, collect, name. Dried plants are enfolded in your pages—the better, we know, to catch fire: memories of the living (those who live are those who fight, proclaimed the old poet), a small heritage of outcasts (their hero is our scoundrel).

The dead haunt only the fabulist minds of the living: "Here lies" obstructs the imagination, "Here lived" stimulates it. Flies drop their eggs off, and then maggots, feasting on tissues, leave behind a jumble of bones—of their dust, soon enough, we shape arrows to let fly at the walls of the warren that is our life.

The Union called for the union of French and colonized workers, and that made sense; the intelligence services drew up a list of each and every subscriber to *Le Paria* and broke into Nguyên's home when he was out, adding notes to those that, for almost three years now, had piled up without any idea, undoubtedly, that they would one day end up in harmless cardboard boxes; the spied-upon defended the Irish cause at the Sorbonne, responded to an increasing number of appeals from any and all, and joined an anarchist meeting as a card-carrying Bolshevik; the spied-upon, again, met Colette and Maurice Chevalier, you're not entirely sure how, but you know that he would keep a soft spot for the singer once his exile had become but a cherished memory; the spied-upon, still him, marched for Sacco and Vanzetti and commemorated the death of Louise Michel: in the month of April 1922 a report described him as a "very active revolutionary agitator [. . .] for whom no means was too extreme"—the first part of that statement seems apt to you.

A few weeks later, Nguyên was fired by his new employer, 65 rue Balagny (today rue Guy-Môquet and a supermarket), because he had taken part, against that employer's will, in May 1 demonstrations. You learn, in another report, that his sister was at the time imprisoned in Indochina for stealing rifles, as was his brother, this time for offering food and lodging to a rebel leader: not being able to stand still is worth more than a family dinner. You also find the exact list of periodicals to which he subscribed, which you'll spare whoever is reading you—let's just say that the man seemed a stranger to frivolity.

Come summer, Nguyên published in the press an open letter penned to the minister of the Colonies. Sarcastic, the author congratulated the colonial authorities for their generosity in Indochina—shootings, repression, exile, the desecration of sacred sites—and praised the "aide-de-camp," pleasant and devoted, that it had hired to ensure a pleasant metropolitan sojourn for militants of the Intercolonial Union. Nguyên nonetheless had one objection to raise: at a time when Parliament intended to save money, was it really sensible to employ decent citizens for such work? Their cost, he explained, weighed on the French nation. In the same tone, the trainee photographer then concluded: since the ministry yearned so very much to know what the Union in general, and its Annamite spokesperson in particular, were doing, they agreed to publish a bulletin every morning so as to inform them of their activities.

This merits the term irony: liberal democracies ended up establishing what no totalitarian regime could have ever put in place: files, updated daily, on every citizen. Paying for a purchase with a card, buying a train ticket, visiting a website, the daily restocking of social media accounts with data: isn't progress exhilarating? You can't stop thinking, as you make your way, about the cameras that capture you at every turn, you and every other passerby, and would've captured Nguyên back then—on a street corner, in the metro, near a library. At least the Annamite had the leisure to escape the snitches that we now enthusiastically keep in our hands at all times. Soon, drones will replace the last birds and facial recognition will expand with no one resisting them at all. Nothing if not banal: comfort rules better than the whip.

The year 1923 began as the last had ended: with the Intercolonial Union monitored at every move. Mid-February, a banquet attracted eighty-three people; mid-March, a meeting on the first floor of a bookshop mustered a crowd of thirty, different people or not, and the revolutionary rose against Platonism, arguing that it was incumbent upon them to act, yes, act; at the end of March, *Le Paria*'s team met to discuss the journal's print run; early April, the editorial team brought up the matter of a member who had apparently used company funds for his own ends; and so on.

The important thing? Nguyên deplored the Union's lack of activity.

And so? And so silence, all of a sudden.

Four years of observation, all for thin air. Disappeared, evaporated, fled. August 3, as thousands gathered in Germany to speak Esperanto, the minister for the colonies sent a letter to the director of the Sûreté Générale: "I have the honor of letting you know that the Annamite known by the name of NGUYEN AI QUOC [. . .] left his home this Jube 13; and si ce that day has not given sign of life. His compatriots and friends seem worried about his disappearance." (Typos in the original.) The man had apparently, according to his own words—words that, as you'd expect, traveled all the way to the Sûreté's ears—left for a brief holiday in Savoy.

Remains, therefore, to track him down; two months would pass in vain.

October 11, a report: the man "is currently in Moscow."

November 19, a report: this "mediocre worker [who] makes a measly living" is "on mission with the Soviets."

A train had taken Nguyên Ai Quôc to Berlin in the early days of summer, furnished with false Chinese papers, bourgeois clothes, a cigar, and a first-class ticket. Granted safe-conduct, in Hamburg he'd boarded a boat sporting the name of a murdered revolutionary; from Petrograd, he had indeed reached Moscow, invited by the Comintern to hone the struggle against the Empire. To his comrades he called brothers, he left a letter saying that while their work hadn't been without merit, it was time to go further still: return to their country, rally the masses, wrest independence. To his nephews, he left a thousand kisses and begged them not to mistreat their little dog. Three decades later, the French state, defeated, would leave Indochina; half a century later, the United States of America, defeated, appended their signature to the bottom of the Peace Accords in Paris, this Paris that the man knew so well and prized perhaps just as much. The man whom no one would again know as Nguyên Ai Quôc had by then been dead for almost four years, after writing in his will, partly censored by the regime, that he had gone to meet up with an old German, an old Russian, and all the old fathers of world revolution.

～

Police block the streets; the CRS are equipped with automatic rifles; two armored vehicles are parked, wire fencing up on a few streets. You walk alongside a barrier. Graffiti garlands the concrete in the colors of insurrection—we'll learn that the sewers by the Élysée Palace were monitored and that a helicopter was dispatched in case its resident had to be extricated ("the Élysée could have fallen," a police officer would later admit openly). A capital rising up, you don't see that every day. Nearby, an armed man tells a distraught tourist, in English, The yellow jackets, they want money, and they don't like our president.

You get to the train station.

Catenary wires, perforated shadows cast across the rails, light brushing against skin and fabric: Paris disappearing in the window frame and the faint hum of a train car.

Thin trunks abandon their reflections on the water's wrinkled green. Sheltered by a shrub that the current cannot carry, five ducks are floating, motionless, by the riverbank. A sixth repeatedly plunges its head in only to raise it back up to the surface. The soft breath of the wind, pushing a few leaves along the current, doesn't muffle the cackling birds.

You pass under a poplar. The whir of litter. Muddy soles. Leaves blotching a wet earth that, ten steps farther, is covered in grass. Rain puddles shimmering: the night made them so that they might penetrate, come daylight, the underbrush— some sprigs point up. Ash and cypress trees grab on to the waxy sky. Not a human soul besides yours; not a sound, besides your boots treading upon the nettles.

The sheep must be in their pen. Their daily presence delights you: marvels of life that, sometimes, venture as close as a few meters. You spare yourself the thought of their future, which shines a light on the whole history of the world.

You approach a hairy oak feasted upon by lichen with

just the right amount of beauty. A dog is rushing about in the distance—without those eyes, tamed, domesticated, by us removed from the pack, the animal would've looked like a wolf. A balloon drifts in the river; a stump, tilted, is half-drowned. It's in these places, yours, that you catch your breath: where silence is sole sovereign; nothing to be sold.

It takes only a rose, said one day the man with rubber sandals, the man of shore and shadows, the pariah whose head was held so high, for all that is arbitrary in the world to cry out in the prisoner's heart.

Winter 2017–Summer 2020

NOTE

I would like to thank Neka here for her map and her inquisitive eye; Élie and Roza, dear fellow travelers; Pip, precious syntactician (take care of yourself); Alain Ruscio, meticulous enthusiast.

All of the books mobilized during my research—brought up, cited, or discussed in these pages—cannot be duly enumerated.

Concerning biographies of Hô Chi Minh, I will nonetheless mention the works of Jean Lacouture (Seuil, 1967), Daniel Hémery (Gallimard, 1990), Thu Trang-Gaspard (L'Harmattan, 1992), William J. Duiker (Hachette Books, 2000), Sophie Quinn-Judge (Hurst & Company, 2003), Pierre Brocheux (Payot, 2003), and Alain Ruscio (Le Temps des cerises, 2019).

Regarding testimonies: *Souvenirs sur Ho Chi Minh* (Hanoi, Foreign Languages Publishing House, 1965), *Ho Chi Minh notre camarade* (Éditions sociales, 1970), *Ho Chi Minh, l'homme et son message* (*Planète Action*, special issue

15, 1970), and *Avec l'Oncle Ho* (Hanoi, Foreign Language Publishing House, 1972).

The title of this work is derived from a poem Hô Chi Minh wrote during his time in China in the 1940s:

> Upon the Range of the West Wind,
> Alone I walk, my heart moved.
> Scanning afar the Southern sky,
> I think of my friends.